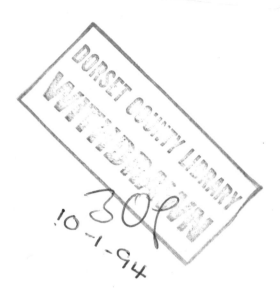

PUFFIN BOOKS

Sam Pig and Sally

'Oh Brock! We've always wanted a tent!' cried the
four little pigs, when Brock the Badger came home one
day with a big exciting bundle on his back, and they
pitched the tent on the high ground where they could
play at rolling downhill.
'Much nicer than an old mouldy house!' cried Sam
Pig, the youngest one, washing the cups in the stream
and leaving them on the bank to dry.
'Much nicer than a stupid old kitchen,' said Bill,
throwing wood on the fire. But, all the same, when
things got scary in the night, with banshees howling,
the four little pigs were only too happy to scuttle
back to the safe little straw-thatched cottage that
was home for all of them!
Altogether it was a happy and fascinating world Sam
Pig lived in, with old friends like Sally the mare and
the Irish cook at the great house to visit, his old enemy
the Fox to outwit, market and May days for variety,
and even hobgoblins and water-maids and enchanted
princesses for friends. For this engaging and
enterprising Pigwiggin lived in the days when streams
and farmhouses still brimmed with living magic.
The other collections of Sam Pig stories in Puffins are
*Adventures of Sam Pig, Yours Ever, Sam Pig, Sam Pig at
the Seaside* and *Sam Pig Goes to Market*. Alison Uttley's
other Puffin books for young readers are *Little Red
Fox, More Little Red Fox Stories, The Little Knife Who Did
All the Work, Magic in My Pocket* and *Adventures of
Tim Rabbit*, and there are two books for older readers,
A Traveller in Time and *The Country Child*.

Alison Uttley

Sam Pig and Sally

Illustrated by A. E. Kennedy

Puffin Books
in association with Faber and Faber

Puffin Books, Penguin Books Ltd, Harmondsworth, Middlesex, England
Penguin Books, 625 Madison Avenue, New York, New York 10022, U.S.A.
Penguin Books Australia Ltd, Ringwood, Victoria, Australia
Penguin Books Canada Ltd, 2801 John Street, Markham, Ontario, Canada L3R 1B4
Penguin Books (N.Z.) Ltd, 182–190 Wairau Road, Auckland 10, New Zealand

First Published by Faber and Faber 1942
Published in Puffin Books 1979
Reprinted 1981

Set, printed and bound in Great Britain by
Cox & Wyman Ltd, Reading
Set in Monotype Baskerville

To Sam, Tim and Shirley

Contents

Sam's little fist shot out and the length of purple ribbon
somehow slipped into it.

Introduction
and
Sam Pig Goes Camping

Once upon a time, you may remember, four little pigs lived in a cottage together with Brock the Badger, their friend and guardian. The cottage where the pigs lived was thatched with straw, and house-leek grew on the roof. There were white curtains sprigged with daisies at the windows and Ann Pig always left the windows open to let in the air. In the kitchen, where the animals had their meals, there were low chairs and a rocking-chair for Brock. The mats were made of rushes, and leafy branches of beech. It was always cool and green in the house of the little pigs.

In the larder was a stone trough which Tom, who was the cook, filled with good things. It was the store cupboard, and into it went jam puffs, and apple pies, crusty bread and round green herb cheeses.

After breakfast while Ann made the beds and shook up the sheeps'-wool blankets, Tom swept the house and yard with a twiggy birch besom, and Bill the gardener went to his digging, but little Sam Pig ran out to the garden gate and swung backwards and forwards. The gate had rusty hinges, and it squealed exactly like a family of pigs, so it was very companionable for Sam.

When the work was done they shut the door and ran off to the fields to look for mushrooms, to hunt for pignuts and truffles and sweet roots. They filled their baskets with blackberries in the autumn, but in spring they gathered young green nettles for soup, and tender stalks of brambles for sweet-meats.

Everyone knew the four pigs who wandered along the hedgerows – with Sam always the last – who peeped at a throstle's nest, or shouted to scare the rabbits. Sometimes they walked miles to the moorland, where the otters lived in the stream and the ravens built their homes. They cut heather and bound it with stalks and carried it home.

'There's nothing as comfortable as heather for a bed,' said Ann, taking the pale purple flowers and stuffing the mattresses. The springy heather was better than a feather-bed, so she filled the beds anew and draped the blankets over them for the night.

In the evening they played games. They raced in the twilight, or played hide-and-seek among the trees. When the stars came out and the moon rose behind the hill, they sat on the doorstep with Brock the Badger. Then Sam played a tune on his fiddle, and Brock told them stories of all the brave little animals he had known in his long life. He spoke of rabbits that defied weasels, and hens that attacked hawks, of dogs that fought wolves. All the little pigs felt a warm brave feeling steal through their bones. They said they would never be afraid.

One day Brock the Badger came home with a bundle on his back. All the pigs came to see what he had brought.

'It's the feather-bed you gave Brock at Christmas for his castle in the woods,' said Bill to Sam.

'It's a bed-quilt,' said Ann to Tom.

Brock said nothing at all. He unrolled the bundle and spread it on the grass. It was a green cloth woven from nettle-flax, so finely made it was like linen. It was strong and stout and there was never a sting left in the nettles.

Brock fetched a couple of sticks and pushed them into the ground. He stretched the nettle cover over them to form a tent and he held the flap open for the family to enter.

'Oh Brock! We've always wanted a tent,' they cried, as they crept into the little green house. 'Ever since we went to the Flower Show in that white tent we've wanted one for ourselves. Can we live in it, Brock? Can we sleep here?'

'Steady on!' laughed Old Badger. 'Not so many questions. You can sleep in it and take it to the fields and go a-camping. Would you like that?'

'Can we? Oh, can we?' The little pigs capered round the tent and danced out of the door with such vigour they nearly upset the slender sticks.

The next day they set off, with Tom carrying the green-nettle tent, Bill dragging a few blankets, Ann following with the frying-pan, and kettle, and Sam with the box of matches. Badger had business with Jack Otter up the river and he left them to camp by themselves. They walked across the fields and up the hills till they found a suitable place. It was a stretch of soft grass near the stream, with a hawthorn bush where they could hang up their belongings, and a rock where they could play. The ground was sloping, but that didn't matter. They liked rolling downhill. So they pitched the tent and collected sticks and boiled the kettle on the fire. Sam ran to the meadow where a red cow was grazing, and he milked it into a tin mug. It was all very homely and comfortable as well as exciting to see the green tent on the hillside waiting for them.

'Much nicer than an old mouldy house,' cried Sam, washing the cups in the stream and leaving them on the bank to dry.

'Much nicer than a stupid old kitchen,' said Bill, throwing wood on the fire.

'I don't know why we live in a house,' said Tom. 'This is much better. Let's stay here always.'

They paddled in the stream and built a dam across it. They sat on the short warm grass and dried themselves. They watched the sun go down, but a chill wind blew over the hill and they decided to go to bed. They wrapped the blankets round their bodies, and soon they were all asleep.

Their snores came squeaking through the tent, and a Great Owl, out on his hunting expedition, heard them. He flew up on silent wings and sat on the hawthorn above the green tent.

'Too-whoo! Too-whoo!' He hooted and cried and wailed. 'There's something queer below. It's those four little pigs! I'll teach them a lesson. Fancy daring to camp in my kingdom when they have a house of their own. They'll scare all the night creatures, and I shall get no supper.'

So the Owl screeched and cried in his most mournful tones. His wife came from the woods, floating like a white shade over the fields, and she cried with him. Such a dismal chorus of sorrow they kept up, it awoke little Sam Pig.

'Did you hear that, Tom?' he whispered, shaking his brother. 'I can hear a banshee crying. Oh Tom, I'm scared.'

'What's a banshee?' asked Ann, creeping up to her brother, and clutching him.

'It's a Goblin, as comes and wails at night,' said Sam. 'The Irishmen told me about it. They've got them in Ireland, and maybe this one has flown over to us. I'm scared.'

'Don't let us stay any longer,' implored Bill and Tom. 'Let's go home.'

'Yes, let's,' wept Ann.

'We said we were going to be brave,' murmured Sam, shaking with fright.

'There isn't time to be brave,' whispered Tom. 'Let's go now. One of them is sitting on the tent pole.'

They peered out and saw the white shapes of the owls. With a wild shriek the four little pigs rolled through the doorway and scampered as fast as they could down the fields to their home. They flung open the door and rushed upstairs.

'Never again will we go camping,' they told each other. 'Wait till Brock comes and we'll tell him all about it.'

At daybreak Brock returned and he was astonished to find the camping party was over, and the tent left on the hill with a pair of banshees in possession.

'Seems to me you're not as brave as I thought,' said he. 'I'll find out what was the trouble. Banshees don't come to torment good little piglings.'

He walked up the fields and there was the tent, just as the pigs had left it, but on its roof lay a white owl's feather and under the hawthorn was a small furry scrap of a mouse.

''Twas only a pair of owls, out on their night hunting,' explained Brock. 'They wouldn't have harmed you.'

'Only a pair of owls! And we ran away,' sighed Sam. 'I did want to be brave.'

'We will go again tonight,' said Ann. 'It was

lovely except for the banshees – I mean the owls.'

'Yes. We will go again, and nothing shall scare us away,' agreed the others, puffing out their chests proudly.

Early in the evening they went back to the tent. They played in the field and made their supper of pignuts which they dug out of the grass. They ate the sweet roots and sprinkled a little salt on them.

That is the nicest supper imaginable if eaten on a hillside with a stream near.

They watched the sun go down, and then they went to bed. They wrapped their blankets around them and snuggled close together. They fell fast asleep, and soon they were snoring and dreaming as all good pigs should dream.

The Fox heard the sound of their snoring as he stepped lightly over the rocks seeking his supper. He came walking delicately, with nose uplifted towards the green-nettle tent.

'Who's this? Who is intruding in my kingdom?' he muttered. 'It's a brass band, trumpets and horns and cornets squeaking. No, it's that family of pigs! I'll give them a lesson! Fancy daring to sleep out on the hillside! They'll warn all the rabbits I'm here. I'll larn 'em.'

The Fox drank up the cold air as if it were water. He filled his lungs with a deep breath, and he lifted a corner of the tent and huffed into it.

'Huff-ff-ff!' went he. 'Huff-ff-ff!'

He blew like a gigantic pair of bellows, puffing out his hairy cheeks, stretching his thin ribs till they nearly cracked.

'Huff-ff-ff-ff!' he sent a hot breath into the little green tent with the force of a gale.

Sam Pig awoke and listened.

'Do you hear that, Brother Tom?' he whispered, and he shook his brother till he sat up.

'What's the matter, Sam?' said Tom sleepily.

'There's a huff and a puff coming into the tent,' said Sam warningly. 'Listen! Hark! A huff and a puff, most terrible.'

Ann and Bill awoke and leaped out of the blankets in fear.

'What is that huffing and puffing, like a giant breathing?' they asked.

'It's a wolf,' said Sam solemnly, and they all opened wide their eyes and crept close to one another.

'Huff-ff-ff! Puff-ff-ff!' hissed the Fox.

'I wish I was at home, safe in my own little bed, with a good roof over me instead of this flimsy tent,' said Ann Pig.

'Oh! Oh!' she cried, as the Fox gave another blast which blew the blanket away. 'Oh, I can't stay here! It's a wolf I'm certain, and I won't stay to be eaten. I'm going.'

'So are we,' muttered the brothers, and they rolled out of the tent and ran all the way home as fast as they could. They dashed into the house and scampered up to bed.

'Never again will we go camping,' they told each other. 'When Brock comes home we will tell him what happened.'

At dawn Brock the Badger returned, and there in the beds lay four little pigs fast asleep. He was surprised to find the camping party over and the tent left behind for a wolf to have.

'Seems to me you're not very brave,' he remarked, looking at them sadly. 'I'll go and find out what happened. Wolves don't huff at little pigs nowadays.'

He walked up the hills to the tent and there it was, just as the little pigs had left it. By the door was a rabbit skin, and the track of the Fox's pads.

'"Twas only the Fox out hunting,' said Brock. 'He paid a visit to you. He wouldn't have harmed you.'

'Only the Fox and we ran away,' groaned Sam. 'It sounded different in the dark. I really must be braver than this.'

'We'll go again tonight,' said Ann. 'I loved the games under the stars and the supper in the open, and the cool air. I shall be brave tonight.'

That evening they went camping again. They played hide-and-seek in the bracken, and paddled in the stream. They made their supper of cresses and sorrel, and they ate the green salad with dandelion and burnet leaves. It was the nicest supper they remembered.

They watched the sun go down and the stars come out and then they went to bed. They wrapped themselves up in their woolly blankets and cuddled close. They fell asleep and soon they were snoring and dreaming in sweet content.

Now William the Bull was walking up the pasture for a drink at the stream, and when he heard that strange snoring sound he stopped and listened.

'There's somebody here,' said William, and he

slowly lowered his great head with its long horns. He lifted the tent high in the air to see who was underneath.

All the little pigs awoke with shrill cries when their roof went away. In the dim light they could see the great black Bull towering over them waving the tent like a handkerchief.

'Quick! Run for your lives,' shouted Sam, 'A monster! A giant!' and the four pigs were off in a jiffy.

The Bull stared after them and then lowered the tent.

'Nay,' said he to himself. 'They didn't wait to see who it was. I only wanted to find out what was underneath. I meant no harm.'

The pigs were already scampering across the fields and woodland home. They threw open the door, rushed upstairs and were in their own beds in a twinkling.

'Never again will we go camping,' they said. 'Wait till Brock comes home and we will tell him.'

When Brock came home there was the little family asleep and the tent left behind on the hillside with a monster of a giant.

'It appears to me you are not brave at all,' said Brock, shaking his head at them. 'You didn't even wait to find out who it was. Away you ran like frightened rabbits. I'm ashamed of you. I'll go and find out what was the trouble. Tents aren't destroyed by giants.'

He walked up the fields and there under the hawthorn stood the black Bull William, trying to straighten out the little tent.

'I'm afraid I've made a hole in this, Badger,' he said. 'I just lifted it to see who was underneath, and your young friends scampered away as if they thought I was going to eat them.'

Brock mended the tent and put it up again, and stayed for a friendly chat with the Bull.

Then he went home to the family.

'It was only William the Bull, going for a drink. He lifted your tent out of curiosity. He never thought he would frighten you away.'

'We weren't brave at all,' sighed Sam. 'I think we shall never be really brave.'

'Let's go again,' said Ann. 'This time we will face any perils. Nothing shall scare us away.'

'Yes, we'll go tonight and face anything that comes,' agreed the others. 'Neither Owls or Foxes or Bulls shall frighten us.'

Once more they went back to the tent on the hillside. They played Ticky-ticky-touchwood among the trees, and rolled down the slopes like barrels. They made their supper of the young green shoots of briars. Stripped of their thorns and eaten like barley-sugar, they are delicious as all country folk know.

They watched the sun go down and the stars come out. Then they went to bed. They wrapped their blankets around them and snuggled close together. Soon they were asleep, and snoring, dreaming good dreams as all little piglings should.

Up the fields came the poacher. He had a bag on his back and snares in his pocket and a cudgel in his hand. He stepped light-footed over the grass towards the plantation where the pheasants were reared. He set his snares for rabbits and left them in the grass. He passed near the stream and suddenly he stopped.

'Help! Help! Murder!' shouted the poacher.

The shrill squeak of the little pigs' snoring came like the sound of bagpipes.

'Who's this? Who's in this tent? There's somebody hiding here. It's my belief it's the keeper on the watch for me. Well, he shan't get me, for I'll be first,' he thought rapidly.

He raised his cudgel and struck the tent a blow. Luckily he hit the frying-pan, and the clatter awoke the little pigs.

'Quick! There's somebody attacking us,' they cried.

'It's a man,' said Sam, peeping out. 'He's got a thick stick ready to fight us. Let's all go for him at once.'

So out of the tent scuttled the four pigs. One ran between the poacher's legs and threw him down. Another drummed on his head with little hard hoofs. Another caught his legs and the fourth danced on his arms.

'Help! Help! Murder!' shouted the poacher, struggling against all the little arms and legs that tried to hold him. 'I'll be off. I'll go.'

He dragged himself free and raced down the hill, over the river back to the village.

'I've been attacked by a whole lot of them; a crowd of them got me down, but I got away,' he told his wife. 'They were in the littlest tent you ever saw. It was hardly big enough for one, but a crowd came out of it, sprottling over me with dozens of arms and legs. I was main glad to escape I can tell you. I shall never go poaching up there again.'

The little pigs took a drink of water from the stream and then went back to sleep.

In the morning they were wakened by the cuckoo, and they had their bathe in the spring water. They ate their breakfast of leaves and they gathered a bunch of water-flowers for Brock. They packed the tent and trotted softly along the paths, gaily talking of their adventure. They all felt nice and warm inside, for they had become brave.

'Well, you didn't run home last night,' remarked Brock, when they strolled into the house. 'I suppose you had a quiet night.'

'No. It was the most exciting time of all, Brock. A poacher came and tried to hurt us, but he only dinted the frying-pan.'

'And, Brock, we drove him away. We unfastened his snares this morning and freed the animals. Yes, we drove him off, at a great rate.'

'So you've found the secret of being brave at last,' said Brock. 'What is it?'

'It's not to run away before you're hurt,' said Sam.

'It's to face things and not turn your back,' said Ann.

'Well, I shall go camping with you tonight,' said Brock. 'Now you have learned not to be afraid I shall go with you. I've seen a nice little place, in a flowery meadow with the stream near and violets like a carpet on the grass.'

So there they camped among the flowers on the meadow, and for many a summer night they slept in the nettle tent. Although many a woodland creature came to sniff and peer at them, they were not frightened again, for they had learned their lesson.

Sam Pig and Sally

'Of course you can't go to market, Sam,' said Bill Pig to his small brother.

'Why not?' asked Sam, kicking at the garden gate and frowning.

'Because you are wanted at home. There's the potato patch to dig, and water to carry.'

'And weeding to be done,' added Tom Pig, removing Sam from the gate. The brothers felt cross, and even the magpie perched on the wall flicked its long tail at him.

'Why do you want to go to market, Sam?' asked Ann.

'Because it was such fun last time,' said Sam. 'I got a ride in the farmer's cart and I saw a monkey and a mouse there.'

Just then Brock came out of the cottage. He walked slowly across the grass. There was an important air about him, and all the pigs stopped arguing at once. The Badger carried his knapsack, and his stick. He was smoking his little pipe of baccy made from Old Man. He stooped and filled his baccy pouch from the fragrant bush by the path. Then he turned to the watching pigs.

'Sam,' said he, 'I want somebody to go to the village with me. You were very successful the last time you went, so I have decided to take you, for it's market day.'

'Oh, Brock! I was just saying, Brock – I was just asking —' stammered Sam.

'There's some weeding to be done,' said Bill.

'Weeding?' Brock opened wide his eyes. 'Who's the gardener, pray tell me? Isn't our Bill the gardener?'

'Yes,' said Bill, sulkily.

'Go and get ready, Sam. We'll start in the flick of the magpie's tail,' said Brock, and he pointed to the black and white bird.

How Sam rushed! He dived into the bowl of water, and scrubbed dirty face and hands. He dived into his coat. Ann brushed his hoofs and gave a twist to his tail. The magpie flicked its wing as Sam came running down the garden path to old Brock. Brock, who had been having a word with the others, turned and regarded the tidy pink-faced little pig.

'Have you a clean handkerchief, Sam?' he asked.

'Yes, Brock,' said Sam, and he dragged it from his pocket, where careful Ann had stuffed it at the last moment.

'Then off we go,' said Brock, and the two animals marched down the lane together.

'Well,' muttered Bill. 'Of all the lucky pigs! Here am I left to do the weeding, and that young varmint goes off with Brock.'

'He weeded yesterday, Bill,' Ann reminded him. 'He hasn't been in a scrape for hours, and he did want to go.'

'He'll get in a scrape there, sure enough,' said Bill sourly, and he stooped to weed the wild strawberries.

Sam and Brock kept to the field paths, avoiding the road where the carts rolled and horses trotted. There were more things to see in the narrow shady green tracks, and Badger pointed out the birds and beasts and hidden homes of tiny creatures. Butterflies, bees, beetles, shrews and hedgehogs all had their homes in the green villages under the hedges. Brock showed Sam cruel Mr Nettle and kind Mrs Dock, growing side by side, the Nettle ready to sting, and the Dock to cure. He showed him the Balsam, a storehouse of little guns ready to be fired. Sam picked here a blue feather, there a round pebble, here a wisp of sheep's wool, there a golden petal.

'What are we going to do at the market, Brock?' asked Sam. 'Are we going to the stalls? I haven't got a penny this time, but I should like to see everything.'

'I'll tell you a secret,' said Brock.

'What is it?' cried Sam, hopping and skipping with excitement.

'It's Ann's birthday tomorrow, and I am going

to buy her a blue ribbon. A real blue ribbon, not made of grass, but of silk.'

'A blue ribbon.' Sam sighed with happiness. 'What's a blue ribbon for, Brock?'

'Not to tie up her bonny brown hair,' laughed Brock. 'It's to hang round her neck with a little locket I've got for her dangling on it.'

'Oh, Brock!' cried Sam, capering round the good old Badger. 'What's a locket, Brock?'

'I'll show you, Sam.' Brock stopped under the hedge and brought out from his pocket a tiny locket made of a walnut-shell, polished and bright. He opened it and inside the little box where the nut had once been there was a peepshow of flowers.

'Oh, how lovely! Ann will like that,' exclaimed Sam, seizing the little treasure-box.

'The flowers won't fade,' Brock told him. 'I have dipped them in dew from Midsummer, to keep them fresh for ever.'

He put the walnut locket back in his pocket and the two went along, jog-trotting at an even pace. Brock jingled a shilling in his pocket and puffed at his pipe and hummed a song. Sam ran here and there like a little dog who is out for a ramble, ever returning to his master's side.

They passed the gateway of the field where the four pigs once went to a Flower Show. All was quiet in the green meadow, and there was no sign of tent or band or crowd.

'Do you remember that brass band?' asked Sam. 'It was lovely music. I do wish we could have a brass band to come and play to us.'

'I don't,' said Brock shortly.

They passed the iron gates and lodge of the Big House.

'Do you remember how I went there once and tumbled into a plum-pudding, Brock?' asked Sam, staring up the drive.

'I do indeed, Sam. You gave us a fright,' answered Brock, grinning at the thought of Sam in the pudding-cloth.

They came to the edge of the village and Sam spoke again.

'Do you remember how I was made a Guy Fawkes, Brock?' he asked, his eyes twinkling.

'I do, Sam. And mind we have no nonsense today. No plum-puddings, or Guys or Flower Show for us today. We are here on serious business, and you must behave yourself like a respectable member of society.'

'Yes, Brock,' said Sam, demurely, but his eyes couldn't help winking. He trotted sedately at Brock's side, and nobody knew that a little Pig and a Badger were walking there.

They went by the barber's shop, and Sam nudged Brock.

'That's where Farmer Greensleeves was shaved,' said he. 'Would you like a shave, Brock?'

'I would not,' said Brock sternly. 'Would you?'

Sam laughed and peeped through the door. 'Farmer Greensleeves is inside now, sitting in a big chair all lathered,' he whispered.

'Come along, Sam. We must go carefully now,' warned Brock.

They went across the market square, where the little wooden stalls had been set up on trestles for the market. Barley-sugar and caraway cakes were heaped on the tables. Baskets of new brown eggs and plump chickens and bloomy plums lay on the edges of the pavement. People walked up and down, tasting and trying, and sampling the fare before they spent their money.

The cheesemonger held out a morsel of cheese from his store of great round cheeses. It was on the point of a knife.

'Taste it. You needna' buy. Just taste my prime cheese,' he cried, so Sam tasted.

'Cheshire cheese,' said Sam, but Brock called to him.

'Come along,' said he. 'There's a ribbon stall across the way. Come along and choose Ann's ribbon. We are not going to hang the locket on cheese.'

They stepped up to the ribbon stall, and there they beheld such a wonderful display they felt helpless to choose.

'Spoilt for choice,' murmured Brock. Ribbons

pink and purple, silver and gold, blue and scarlet, hung from the wooden rail.

They were curled like serpents, and they fluttered like flags. They dipped like feathers, they swung like leaves.

'I want a sky-blue ribbon,' said Brock in his best voice.

'Sky-blue ribbon,' echoed Sam in his high squeak, which so startled the fat woman who kept the stall she nearly dropped her scissors.

'Sky-blue ribbon,' said Brock again in his deep bass.

'Blue heaven ribbon,' squeaked Sam.

'Sky-blue heaven ribbon,' echoed the confused woman, and she glanced sharply at them. Queer little customers whose voices were so odd! She showed them her broad ribbons and her narrow ones, and Brock chose a medium-sized one, delicate as the noon-day sky.

'What do you think of this?' he asked Sam Pig.

Little Sam nodded his head. He liked all the ribbons. They grew on the stall like flowers at the Flower Show. There was a purple ribbon that gave him such joy his mouth watered. It was like stormy thunder clouds and foxgloves.

'Fivepence change,' said the stall-keeper. She looked in her money-box for the change. Sam's little fist shot out, and the length of purple ribbon some-how slipped into it. Like water the shimmering satin fell and Sam draped it under his coat, next to his heart.

'Thank you, ma'am, and good day,' said Brock, touching his cap politely, and Sam too said, 'Thank you very very much, ma'am.'

'Funny customers,' said the woman. 'Ugly, but folk can't help their faces. A regular little pig face had that boy.'

The Badger and Sam Pig crossed the market, stopping now and then to listen to a huckster, or a quack selling pills. Brock gave Sam a penny to spend and he bought some pear drops for the family at home. Poor old Bill, weeding the garden, and poor old Tom, leaning on a gate, and poor Sister Ann darning a hole in Sam's everyday coat. How nice it was to be Sam Pig with yards of purple ribbon in his coat front! Sam gave a skip and a hop. Then he spied Sally the mare, with Farmer Greensleeves, freshly-shaven, sitting in the cart.

'Hello, Sally,' he squealed, and everybody looked round. Sam pretended he knew nothing about that shrill squeak that had rung through the market-place.

'Silence!' muttered Brock. 'Keep quiet while I go and look at those rope ends. I could do with a bit of rope.'

But Sally had heard Sam's voice, and she wriggled her ears and glanced sideways at him. The farmer stopped and climbed down. He tied the reins to the

brake and went across to a stall for a pound of candy.
Sam stepped quickly up to the mare.

'Oh, Sally, here we are, Badger and me! We've
come to market for a secret.'

'Have you really?' asked Sally, rolling her eyes.
'I've come to bring the eggs, four hundred of them,
and the butter that Mollie made, and the big round
cheeses.'

'Sally,' said Sam, in a confidential whisper.
'Would you like a birthday present? Is it your
birthday, Sally?'

'It may be, and then it may not,' said Sally,
cautiously.

Sam brought from under his coat yards and yards
of shining purple ribbon and twined it round Sally's
collar like a wreath of foxgloves. It hung among the
horse-brasses, the sun and moon and star, it fell over
the little tinkling bell, it swayed in the great leather
collar and dropped over the shafts of the cart, like a
beautiful set of reins.

'You do look a treat, Sally,' said Sam, admiringly.
'How old are you today?'

'I'm supposed to be twenty-one,' said Sally.
'But I feel like a two-year-old.'

The old mare tossed her head and jingled the
golden brasses, so that the sun and crescent moon and
spiky star sparkled. The little bell chimed, and the
ribbons fluttered round her patient long face.

'What the—? Who the—? What the dickens is

this?' cried the astonished farmer, who chanced to look round to see if the mare was standing steady. He walked quickly back to her, and the people nearby all laughed.

'A regular May day mare, Farmer Greensleeves,' said they.

'Going to the Royal Show?' asked a wag.

'Or is it Coronation Procession?' asked another.

'It's that little Sam Pig, who's been up to something,' murmured the farmer, and Sam smiled up at him. 'What are you doing, Sam?'

'It's Sally's birthday,' explained Sam. 'She's two-years-old.'

'That she isna'. She's no two-year-old, isna' our Sally. She was born on March the fifth, twenty-one years ago, the same day as my eldest son.'

Then Brock came along. He had swapped a little Badger hair brush, made from his combings, for the rope end, and he swaggered along, very proud of his purchase. He saw Sam talking to Sally and the farmer, but when he got near, the fountains and the cascades of ribbons dazzled his eyes.

'What's this? Where did you get that ribbon, Sam?' he asked sternly.

'That's what I asked, Mister Brock,' said the farmer.

'Sam. Did you take it from the ribbon stall?'

'Yes. There was plenty left,' said Sam airily. 'More ribbon than honeysuckle in the hedge. More than roses on a bush. So I tooked it.'

'Sam! Sam! You said you would be good,' reproved Brock, sadly.

> 'He that takes what isn't his'n
> Will find 'isself inside a prison,'

said the farmer.

Brock and the farmer unwound the ribbon and twisted it in a neat coil. Sally looked quite down-hearted, and Sam's eye had a tear in the corner.

'Take it back to the market-woman,' said Brock, 'and give her these pennies I have left. Tell her you are sorry.'

So Sam carried the coil of ribbon away to the stall. He said his apologies quickly, and laid the money with it. Then without waiting to hear what the woman said, he hurried back to Brock.

'Come along home now,' said Brock. 'We've done enough for today. We shall just be in time for tea if we walk quickly.'

'Don't tell about the ribbon, Brock,' said Sam, as they sped along the road.

'All right. I won't tell,' said Brock kindly.

'She did look beautiful, didn't she, Brock?'

'Yes,' said Brock.

'I shall make a wreath of something else,' Sam went on. 'I could get some foxgloves and poppies perhaps and make a garland for her neck.'

'Yes,' said Brock. 'That would be better.'

Then they talked of the walnut locket, and they threaded the ribbon though the little holes in the shell ready for the birthday.

'And what happened at the market?' asked Bill, when they were all having tea.

'It was as usual,' said Brock. 'Ribbons and laces, and sweet pretty faces, but never a face as sweet as Ann's.'

'Stuff and nonsense,' muttered Bill.

'Did you see anything of Farmer Greensleeves and Sally?' asked Tom Pig.

'Yes, they were there, and Sally looked wonderful. She had had her twenty-first birthday recently, but she looked only two-years-old,' said Brock, with a little glance at the blushing Sam.

'I love Sally,' said Sam, with a gulp.

The next day Brock gave little Ann Pig the walnut locket, hanging on its sky-blue silk ribbon. All the pigs came to see her unfasten it. The flowers inside were bright as the sun, and the Midsummer dew glittered on their petals like diamonds.

'What a lovely present,' cried Ann. 'Look at the ribbon. Look at the catch on the locket, how it shuts up tightly. Isn't it beautiful! Thank you very much, Brock.'

She hung it round her neck and there was nobody more happy in all the world that morning than little Ann Pig, unless it was her brother Sam.

Sam Pig and the
Hurdy-gurdy Man

The little country road linked village to hamlet, and along it travelled farmers' carts, wagons, horses, and ordinary people going about their daily business. Fields stretched on either side, with hedges of wild roses and bitter-sweet, with ditches of meadowsweet and rushes. The road ran like a white ribbon in the green countryside.

Along this road one summer's day there came a small figure in check trousers and wide sun-hat. By his way of walking anyone could recognize little Sam Pig. Usually Sam took the field paths, the tracks used by animals, the lonely ways where the only folk one would meet were foxes and hedgehogs and tramps and pedlars and farm men. This day Sam went on the road for a special reason. He walked at a good pace, keeping close to the hedge, singing a song, dancing a few steps now and then, calling to bird and beast in the field.

The hedge came to an end, and a low stone wall began. It was a very old wall, green with stonecrops and ferns, rosy with Robin-run-in-the-hedge, and purple with toad flax. The flowers made a patchwork of colour on the ancient wall. The stones were bound together by a tangled web of roots and flowers which had grown there undisturbed for a hundred years.

Sam Pig sat down on this little wall. It was so low he could rest his feet on the ground. It was as comfortable as an easy chair, with its mossy-cushioned stones.

Sam took a small notebook and a pencil from his pocket.

He was going to write down all the things that passed along the road that morning. He sat there waiting, watching the bend in the road. It was very quiet, with only the sound of the river murmuring as it fell over the distant rocks, and the hum of the insects in the grasses.

Sam licked the pencil and waited. After a long time a cart came slowly along the road, and Sam wrote down 'cart'. Next came a high-wheeled yellow gig with a prancing horse, well groomed and beautiful. Sam noted it in his book, in his own special writing. After another long wait came an ancient motor car, and then a donkey-cart. So the country traffic moved along that winding road among wild roses and violets, and some people nodded to Sam, and cried 'How'do?' and others never saw him at all. He sat very still, like a part of the lichened mossy wall, intent on his work, and naturally it took a long time to write each word.

Of course Sam didn't write as you and I write, for he had never been to school. He made little pictures, which were just as good as words and twice as nice. There was a square cart for the farmer's cart, and a long cart for the brewer's dray, and a couple of little wheels for a bicycle. The best word was the donkey-cart, but Sam made a rag-bag for a beggar who lurched past and a sunbonnet for a little girl who dawdled along with many a backward glance at little Sam sitting on the wall.

Well, Sam made the list, and he was thinking of going home to show it to Brock when somebody else came along the road. It was a humped figure who limped very slowly.

'I'll wait for this one and then I'll go,' said Sam, licking his pencil hopefully. He had seen neither wizard nor fairy nor giant. They don't walk the highroads in these days, and Sam was curious about this creature coming. Then Sam saw that the hump was a kind of box the stranger carried, slung on his shoulder by a strap. There was a wooden leg attached to it. Sam was so much excited over this box, with its painted front, that he forgot to write anything in his book.

The man came up to him and stopped. He slipped the strap from his shoulder and took off his old green hat. He looked very tired, and dusty.

'A hot day, mate,' he remarked. 'Hot work carrying all this 'ere.'

'Yes, sir,' said Sam.

'Can you guess what this is?' continued the man.

'No, sir,' said Sam.

'It's a hurdy-gurdy. Have you ever seen a hurdy-gurdy, my lad?'

'No, sir,' said Sam, his eyes popping with wonder.

The man sat down on the wall by Sam's side. He wiped his face and neck with his red handkerchief, and Sam saw how thin and weary he was.

'I could do with a drink. I'm parched. How far is it to the next village, mate?' asked the man.

'A few miles,' said Sam. 'I could get you a drink if you've got a cup, sir.'

The man opened a sack and took out an enamel mug. Sam ran off to the field close by where there was a spring of fresh cold water, icy from the depths of the earth. He carried it carefully to the thirsty hurdy-gurdy man.

'Thank you. Thank you, mate. I've not tasted water like this spring water since I was a little nipper like you living in the country,' said the man. Then he hesitated and peered at Sam more closely.

'Well, not like you, for I must say you've got big ears and an uncommonly ugly face.'

'Yes, sir,' said Sam.

The man drained the mug and put it away.

'Now, for that little attention, I'll tell you what I'll do. I'll play you a tune on my hurdy-gurdy. Would you like that?'

'Oh yes, sir,' said Sam, clapping his hands.

So the man put the wooden leg under the hurdy-gurdy and turned the handle. Such a jolly tune came rippling out, in a fountain of little notes, Sam could hardly keep himself from dancing. But the lovely

music went wrong, it stammered, and some notes dropped away, and others ran into one another. The hurdy-gurdy was old, its tunes were cracked, its best days were done. It tried hard, but it couldn't manage. It was a pity, for it was a very nice old hurdy-gurdy.

'Well, I must be going, mate,' said the man, rising slowly to his feet. 'I'm tired and I could sit here all today and all tomorrow. I could sleep here.'

'Why don't you?' asked Sam.

'I've got my living to earn, my bread and cheese and drop of beer.'

He hoisted the box on his shoulder, and took up the sack. He looked so tired Sam was sorry for him.

'Would you like someone to help you?' asked Sam timidly.

'Well, I should, but I can't pay anything. I've taken nothing today, and that water is the first drink that has passed my lips. I must get on to the village and earn my meat.'

'I'll go with you,' said Sam. 'I can help a bit.'

So away with the hurdy-gurdy man went Sam. The little pig wasn't afraid, for the man's face was kind.

Sam carried the sack, which held the mug, a clean shirt, and a pair of Sunday trousers. They talked as they went along – at least the man talked and Sam listened. He told Sam about the places he had seen on the road, little stone Cotswold villages, and beautiful towns, and slow-moving rivers, and deep woods. He had played his hurdy-gurdy in every village and now he was moving North to the hills and high moors and wild rivers.

As he talked they came to the gates of the Big House, and they both stared up the drive.

'Will you play there?' asked Sam hopefully. 'If we can get past the lodge safely, we can play to the cook. She's a friend of mine, an Irishwoman.'

The lodge-keeper wasn't in sight, so they went through the massive gates and up the long drive to the Big House. Sam led the way to the back door. The hurdy-gurdy man set up his musical box and turned the handle. The gay, crooked, broken little tunes came tumbling out. They were lovely and they were wrong, tantalizing with their confusion. The cook came to the door, and after her came the two little blue-clad kitchen-maids.

'Glory be, I bethought me 'twas the little pigs squealing here, and they afther being killt,' said she. 'I'll give ye a penny to go away with that hurdy-gurdy of yours, me man.'

Then she caught sight of little Sam Pig, smiling up at her with his wide mouth and innocent blue eyes.

'Arrah! If it isn't the little Pigwiggin! If it isn't the little cratur as fell into the puddin' bowl and got mistook for a Leprechaun an' all! Indade, and it's welcome you are, and plase to forget the hard words I said about your organ there. Your tunes are in need of a plumber, I'm thinking. It's tarrible quare they are, lepping about like a mad Mooley cow.'

'I thought you would like to hear the music,' said Sam, disappointedly.

'Indade an' I do. But if the misthress hears ever a

squeak of it she'll be afther sending you off double quick. So hould your whist a minute while I'm afther getting you a sup of tay and a bite. Come ye in.'

They followed the kind cook down the stone passage to the big kitchen. They sat down by the fire and she made them tea and gave them food. The hurdy-gurdy man ate ravenously, and the cook looked pityingly at him.

'It's famished ye are. You look tired to the bone,' said she.

'Nay, I've got my living to earn. I can't lay up,' said the man.

She got her purse from the kitchen drawer and gave him a few pence. Then she sent him on his way.

'Good-bye, hurdy-gurdy man. Good-bye little Pigwiggin, and God be with you,' said she.

They went down the drive, but the lodge-keeper was waiting for them with angry words. They went to the village, but everybody was too busy to give money to a cracked old hurdy-gurdy. Sam held out the mug and rattled a penny in it, but at the end of the day there was only fivepence in it.

'You'd best be going home, young Sam,' said the hurdy-gurdy man. 'Thank you for your company. You've helped me quite a lot.'

'What will you do, Mister Hurdy-gurdy man?'

'Oh, I shall have a bite and then sleep under the hedge and struggle on,' said the man wearily.

'I know a nice place for you. I know a barn with hay in it. Would you like that?' asked Sam.

'I should indeed,' said the man.

'Then I'll wait while you have your supper and I'll take you there. It's at Woodseats Farm, where Farmer Greensleeves lives. He's a friend of mine, like Sally and all of them.'

'Well, that would suit me down to the ground,' said the man.

He went to the inn and had his bread and cheese. Then he walked back with Sam. This time they went by the little paths, on grass that was soft to the man's feet.

Sam saw the farmer, and he ran across to ask permission.

'Of course, Sam Pig, any friend of yours is welcome,' said Farmer Greensleeves, affably. So Sam took the hurdy-gurdy man to the big barn, and fetched him a mug of milk and a hunch of cake from the farm-house.

'I shall be all right tomorrow, Sam,' said the man, lying down in the sweet-smelling hay. 'A good night will set me up.'

'There's just one thing,' said Sam. 'Will you lend me the hurdy-gurdy for tonight? I want to play to my brothers. I'll bring it back tomorrow.'

'Yes, take it. It's so cracked you can't make it any worse. Take it, Sam,' said the man, and he fell asleep.

Sam staggered slowly away with the hurdy-gurdy

on his back. It took a long time to get home, but he was excited at the thought of the surprise he had in store for Brock and the family.

He walked softly up the path, set up the hurdy-gurdy, and began to play. The door was flung open, and the three little pigs came tumbling out, shrieking with joy.

'Good gracious, Sam! You did startle us! What is this magical box? Oh how lively it is! Let me try,' they called, and they took turns to wind the handle and the little cracked tunes came jumbling out higgledy-piggledy to their delight.

'Sam,' said Brock as he listened. 'It sounds a bit cracked to me.'

'Never mind. We love it,' said the pigs.

'I think that hurdy-gurdy has seen its best days. It must be fifty years old,' said Brock, looking at it.

'We love it,' said the pigs again.

All evening they played, but when the sun went down and they came in to supper, Brock took the hurdy-gurdy to pieces. He worked at it for an hour and then he carried it off to the woods.

'I'll put some new tunes in this hurdy-gurdy,' he thought.

He let the wind blow into it, and the nightingale sing into it. He let the brook murmur by it, and the trees rustle there. Then he brought it back to the house.

The door was flung open, and the three little pigs came
tumbling out.

'Play one more tune before we go to bed,' begged the little pigs.

'All right. Now listen,' said Brock. He turned the handle and the most lovely music came out, far sweeter and clearer than ever before. Nothing cracked or false was left. The Badger had put the music of the woods into the old hurdy-gurdy. There was a nightingale singing in the background, and a blackbird fluting to a song. There was sunshine and May Day in it. There was the harp of the trees, and the murmur of wind and water all mingled with the original airs of the little organ.

'What have you done?' asked Sam. 'It's quite different. It's beautiful now.'

'I've mended it,' said Brock. 'If I can mend broken whistles and broken hearts, I can surely mend a broken hurdy-gurdy.'

Sam carried it back to the barn the next morning. The hurdy-gurdy man was asleep, but he awoke when Sam opened the door and let in a flood of sunshine.

'How have you slept?' asked Sam.

'Champion! I feel a different man. I can face anything now,' said the man, stretching himself and standing up to shake the hay from his hair.

'Let's go to the farm and play them a tune,' said Sam. 'It will please them.'

'Maybe they won't be so pleased when they hear my poor old hurdy-gurdy,' laughed the man ruefully.

They walked across to the farmhouse and the man played the hurdy-gurdy.

'What have ye done to it?' he asked, as he turned the handle. 'Nay, this is a fair treat to listen to. It's all changed. It's better than ever it was. There are the old tunes made lovely. What have ye done?' he asked amazed.

'It was Brock the Badger who did it,' said Sam. 'He mended it for you. He said you would never lack money or friends while you played those tunes, for they will bring back good days to the memory of listeners. He said all the world will want to hear your hurdy-gurdy now.'

It was true. The hurdy-gurdy man never lacked a kind friend and money in his purse. He went through all the villages in England and Ireland, playing his tunes to the people, and giving joy to the listeners. Every year he came back to the farm, and then Sam Pig and Brock the Badger met him and heard his tales, and turned the handle of the little hurdy-gurdy for their own pleasure. Out came the rippling dancing tunes which made the children dance and the women smile in every cottage of the land.

The May Queen

Brock the Badger sat in the kitchen one day of early spring, with the little pigs round him.

'Show us your pocket-book, Brock. Tell us about the feast days coming,' they pleaded.

'It was such a long cold winter,' said Sam. 'I thought it would never end. I'm glad there are feast days.'

Brock took the old leather-backed book from his pocket and turned the pages so that the little pigs could look at the pictures.

'Daffodil day in March,' said Brock. 'And here's April. April Fool's Day, when we all play tricks. Swallow Day, when the first swallow comes. Nightingale Day, when the little brown bird sings. Cuckoo Day, when our old friend flies over the sea to our woods. All those festivals for April.'

'Cowslip Day, when the first cowslip is out,' added Sam Pig, leaning over Brock's shoulder, and pointing to a picture of the flowers painted in gay colours on the brown page.

Brock turned over, and showed them a fine picture with many a gay scene.

'That is a day when men as well as animals have a feast. What is it? Who can tell me?'

'May Day,' they all shouted together.

'Yes, May Day, when the children dance round the Maypole. May Day, when the cart horses are decorated and their shoes blacked and polished. Then Sally the mare will have her mane plaited with straw tassels standing up in a row, and her tail brushed in a wave with little straw plaiting and ribbons down the centre. It's Sally's day too.'

'The cart will be decorated, won't it, Brock?' asked Ann.

'Yes. Everything at the farm will be spick and span, washed and clean, polished and brushed for May Day,' said Brock.

'And everything in the house of the four Pigs must be clean and fresh for May Day too,' said Ann.

'Yes. We'll have a May Day feast like the farm.'

On the Eve of May Day Sam Pig went over to the farm to talk to Sally the Mare. She stood in the stable, while the boy plaited her mane and tail in many plaits to make it curly for the next day. Her fetlocks were washed and combed, her coat groomed. The ribbons and rosettes and straw hung near, ready for May Day. Sam slipped quietly away and went to the cowhouses. He found everyone excited and gay. The cows were going to be let into the big meadow the next morning, and they were talking of the sweetness of the grass there, and the taste of the spring that ran through the field, and the feeling of comfort of the old tree stump where they rubbed their backs and sides. They were looking forward to May Day.

The little pigs in the pig-cote were squealing so loudly they didn't hear Sam's step as he crept up to the wall and looked over at them.

'Oh, Sam! How you startled us!' they cried. 'Do you know what day it is tomorrow?'

'May Day,' said Sam proudly. 'I know!'

'Yes, and we are going to be let into the little orchard, so that we can rootle among the trees. My! It will be a treat after being shut in the pig-cote yard for so long. The grass is thick and cold, and we shall scratch our backs on the trees, and gallop around like circus pigs. We shall dig and wallow to our hearts' content on May Day.'

Sam walked on, to visit the pasture where the sheep and lambs were feeding. The sheep called to their little ones, who frisked and danced on their hind legs like ballet girls.

'Oh, Sam Pig! It's May Day tomorrow,' they bleated. 'Our lambs are going to race from the oak tree to the white gate. It's the May Day race, and for many a year the lambs have run that race.'

'Yes. I can see a little deep path,' said Sam,

looking at the ground where a tiny track led from tree to gate.

'We ran there in our childhood. Our mothers ran too. Now our children are going to race. The winner will be the Queen of the lambs,' said the sheep.

So Sam went through the farm and everywhere he heard tales of the May Day festival.

Then he saw two children coming from the house with a basket. He crouched low under the hedge out of their way, but he could hear their voices ringing across the field with joy.

'We'll gather cowslips and bluebells from Puwit Meadow, and Jack-by-the-hedge from Cuckoo Meadow, and some primroses for my hair,' said the little girl.

'And we'll get some fresh branches of larch for an archway to hold over you, and some young beech leaves too,' said the little boy.

'And daffodils from the riverside, and forget-me-nots if we can find any out yet.'

'And a tulip from the garden, and some wild cherry from the wood,' added the boy.

They ran with skipping steps over the meadow, and the girl began to sing as she picked the blossoms and filled her basket.

'I shall be Queen of the May. I shall be Queen of the May.'

Sam Pig went home thoughtfully.

'What is Queen of the May?' he asked Brock.

'A little girl wears a crown of flowers and garlands. In some places they have a Crowning of the Queen, with dancers and all. They dance round the Maypole and sing a song,' said Brock.

'I should like to be Queen of the May,' said little Ann Pig.

'Yes,' said Sam. 'Ann is our prettiest little girl. She shall be the May Queen.'

'Hurrah!' cried Bill and Tom, as Ann blushed with pleasure. 'Let Ann be Queen of the May.'

'Very well,' said Brock, laughing at their eagerness. 'Ann Pig is our very own Queen of the May.'

At daybreak they were out in the woods to gather fresh flowers and branches with the dew upon them. They carried their trophies back to the garden and wove them into garlands and wreaths. They made a crown of cowslips for little Ann's head. They put a chain of bluebells round her neck. They gave her a bouquet to carry.

'She ought to wear a veil. A Queen has a veil hanging from her head,' said Sam, who knew all about these things.

He ran out and brought home a beautiful cobweb, shimmering with dewdrops. Brock breathed upon it, and the drops glittered like diamonds, with rainbow colours. They draped the web from Ann's crown so that the little gleaming drops hung about her face.

'A Queen! A beautiful Queen! Much prettier than

an ordinary girl,' they cried, bowing to her, and they led Ann to the stream to look at herself.

They gave her a sceptre made of an ivy-covered wand, and twisted an archway of branches to hold over her.

'Am I really a May Queen?' asked Ann as Brock took his pipe out of his mouth to stare at her.

'Realer than real. A grand May Queen, little Ann,' said Brock, and he clapped his hands.

'But where are you going?' he asked as the four

pigs walked down the garden path, Ann leading, with her veil hanging about her, and the others carrying bunches of flowers and the archway of young beech.

'To show ourselves to Sally the Mare, and Rosie the Cow, and perhaps to Mollie the dairymaid, or to Farmer Greensleeves,' they said.

'That's all right,' said Brock. 'I thought you had some other plan in your foolish little noddles.'

They walked across the fields to the farm. In the big meadow the cows were frisking, eating the sweet grass, rubbing their sides against the well-known smooth tree trunk.

'I am the Queen of the May,' said Ann Pig.

The cows glanced at her, and turned away to their feeding, but Rosie, the Red Heifer, ran across the field to admire little Ann.

Quickly Ann picked a bunch of buttercups and wove them into a circlet. She threw the wreath over the cow's horns.

'There, Rosie. You too are a Queen of the May,' said she.

The little procession left the field and went to the pasture where the sheep gathered with their lambs.

'Who is the Queen of the lambs?' asked Ann Pig.

'The race is about to begin,' said a hurried, flustered mother, pushing her twins into the row with the crowd. Off they went, leaping and running, away from the old oak tree across the field to the white gate. Every sheep called to her youngling, and there was such a chorus of Baas it was deafening. The lambs reached the white gate in a mob, and turned round, tearing helter-skelter, tumbling over one another, leaping over a ditch in the way, dancing on their neat little toes, waving their flags of tails.

'Run, little one, run,' cried every mother in the field.

'I am running, mother,' bleated the babies.

A little black lamb was the winner, and it ran to its mother to be nuzzled and petted.

'She shall be Queen of the lambs for May,' said Ann, and she crowned the lamb with a crown of daisies.

Then away went the four little pigs, with Ann in front, wearing her chaplet of cowslips, and the others holding the arch of leaves over her veiled head.

They went to the orchard where the little pigs were rootling, and digging for roots.

'Here's the May Queen,' they cried, when they saw Ann. They all danced round an apple tree, which they called their Maypole, and Ann sat in the low branch singing with them.

Next they went to the farmyard where Sally the Mare was standing, waiting for the farmer and the family. Sally's hoofs were blacked. Her tail was hanging free with a tiny plait of ribbons down the centre. Her frizzed mane was decorated with straw tassels, upright in a nodding row, and little stiff flowers stood between them. She wore all her horse brasses, shining like gold. The harness was clean and bright, and the cart had been washed and decorated with a bunch of flowers on each side.

'Queen Sally and Queen Ann,' said Sam Pig, looking at the mare in deep admiration. 'You are both Queens of the May.'

'There's another Queen coming out in a minute,' said Sally. 'But little Ann Pig is the best of all in my opinion. Of course I'm only an old mare, but I do know something about May Queens, and Ann is a beauty.'

The door opened and the farmer came out, dressed in his Sunday clothes. He carried the long whip with a ribbon tied to the handle. Behind him came the children and Mrs Greensleeves. The little girl was dressed in white. She had a veil of muslin, and on her head a wreath of primroses and lilies. In her gloved hands she carried a large bouquet. She was indeed a proper little Queen of the May, with golden hair and pink cheeks and solemn face. She stared at Ann Pig and Ann Pig stared back. After her ran the little boy, in his stiff Sunday clothes, with white collar and little blue tie. His face was red, polished with soap, and his hair was still wet with the washing he had had. He held a green larch bough, ready to put over his sister when they reached the village.

'Who the—? What the—? Who's this?' stammered the farmer, as he suddenly caught sight of the little pigs standing near Sally. 'Who's this May Queen?'

'Ann Pig, Sam Pig, Bill Pig and Tom,' said Sam, stepping forward.

'Bless my buttons! Bless my bottom sixpence! Bless my boots!' cried the farmer. 'Here's those wild little piglings, looking as nice as my own family. Well done! I'd take you with me to dance round the Maypole, but the cart will be full of us.'

'No, thank you,' said Ann, shrilly. 'I'm Queen of the May here, where I belong. Brock doesn't want us to go wandering.'

'Quite right,' nodded the farmer.

'Wife,' he called to Mrs Greensleeves. 'See here. Give this little May Queen a bite and a sup for May Day presents.'

The farmer's wife brought them cakes and milk and some sweet wizened apples from the apple chamber.

'It's time I was off, Wife,' said the farmer, looking at his turnip watch. 'Come along, childer, and climb in the cart. We shall be late for Maypole dancing if we stay any longer.'

The little girl and boy climbed in, and the farmer's wife squeezed after them. There certainly wasn't room for four little pigs as well.

'Gee up, Sally. Come along Sally lass,' chirruped the farmer, waving his ribboned whip round his head.

The cavalcade started, with jingling of bells and tinkling of brasses, with nodding flowers and plumes and ribbons.

'Good-bye! Good-bye!' called the little pigs.

'A happy May Day,' called the children, and away they went.

'Time to go home,' said Sam. 'Brock will wonder where we are.'

'I wish we could dance round the Maypole,' said Ann, as they set off across the fields, running, with the veil tucked up and the flowers fluttering their petals.

Brock stood at the gate waiting for them, and when they went up the garden path there grew a Maypole in the middle of the grass. It was a tall pole of hawthorn, with flowers covering it, and long ribbons of woven grasses hanging down.

'Each take a ribbon and dance round the Maypole. That's the way to do it. In and out and roundabout,' said Brock.

He took a whistle pipe out of his pocket and whistled a lively air, and the little pigs danced their Maypole dance, twisting the ribbons until they were in a tangle of knots.

They hung their wreaths and crown on the Maypole, and went into the kitchen. What a feast lay there! The good old Badger had been cooking all the time they had been Maying. He had set the table and spread out all the good things for them. There were bannocks and pikelets and oatcakes and barm dump-

'Each take a ribbon and dance round the Maypole.'

lings, fried in the frying pan, baked on the stone girdle, as well as stuffed eggs and apple pie.

'Here's to the May Queen, and may she live long, and dance every May Day till the earth dances too,' said Brock, holding up a glass of cowslip wine and toasting the little May Queen.

'And here's to Old Brock, and may he live forever,' said Sam.

'Here's to all of us, and all of you wherever you are,' said Brock again, and he drank to the whole wide world.

Sam Pig's Egg

There are eggs and eggs in this wide world – good eggs and bad eggs, new-laid and addled, eggs of hens and singing-birds and the soft frog-spawn. There are sea-blue eggs in the hedgesparrow's nest, and greenish blue eggs with brown markings in the blackbird's. Sam Pig knew all these eggs and many another, but he had never seen an egg like the one he found.

The little Pig went out one spring day, hunting in the hedgerows and ditches, in the hawthorn bushes and little trees for eggs. He found plenty, the exquisite gems of spotted and mottled blue, tiny beautiful things that belonged to the birds. Bright eyes watched him fearlessly, and feathered bodies ruffled as he came near.

'No touching! No taking!' they warned him.

'Of course not,' said Sam indignantly. 'I was only looking.'

'There's an egg that belongs to nobody lying among the tombstones in the church-yard,' said a robin to Sam. 'I saw it there this morning. Would you like it?'

'I can't bother going all that way,' said Sam, lazily. 'I can get a hen egg any day from the farm.'

'It isn't a hen egg. You go and fetch it, Sam. It may be a Dodo's egg, for all I know.'

Sam was interested, and he trotted off through the fields and lanes for a few miles to the church-yard. There, on an ancient tomb which lay flat among the thick grasses, was an egg. It was larger than a hen's egg, golden-brown with a gloss like burnished metal, warm with the sun's heat. All was quiet in that garden of peace and Sam picked up the egg and carried it off.

He showed it to his brothers when he got home.

'There's perhaps a fine and beautiful bird inside,' said Tom Pig. 'There may be a real peacock like the one at the Big House, or perhaps a parrot like Widow Waley's,' said Bill Pig.

'Is there a little angel inside?' asked Ann, opening wide her blue eyes as she touched the shining shell. 'They come to church-yards.'

'I've never seen an egg like it,' confessed Brock. 'Never in all the woods and fields and moors have I seen such an egg. We must hatch it, and see what comes out, for it is still warm, and it must have been laid recently.'

'I shall give it to the rooks to hatch,' said Sam. 'Their elms overhang the church-yard. They may know something about it.'

'Who's going to climb those tall trees to put it in their twiggy nests?' asked Bill.

'It would roll out and break on the tombstones,' said Ann, shaking her head. 'Don't give it to the rooks, Sam.'

'They'll eat it,' said Brock. 'A wonder they left it alone in the church-yard. I think you must find somebody else, Sam.'

So Sam put it in the hedgesparrow's nest. The little hedgesparrow thought it belonged to a new kind of cuckoo. She sat on it for a day, perched uneasily on the slippery ball. Then she protested to Sam.

'Take this awful egg away,' she cried. 'I can't balance myself on the top. I keep slipping down. It's too big for my nest.'

'Who will hatch it for me?' asked Sam.

'Try the farmyard. Put it under a broody hen,' suggested the hedgesparrow. 'Hens are used to duck eggs and turkey eggs, and they won't mind this queer thing.'

Sam took the egg to the farmyard. He walked warily, for he didn't want anyone to see the golden-brown egg. The speckled hen with feathers fluffed out agreed to sit on it if Sam would bring her a drink of water and a morsel of corn each day. She sat on it, hidden from the eyes of the farmer, away in a corner of a barn, but nothing happened.

'Sam Pig! Sam Pig!' she cried fretfully. 'I don't like this egg. It is so hard, and heavy. Take it away.'

'Please hatch it for me, speckled hen,' implored Sam, who had visited her each day. 'Do take care of it for me.'

'It's no use, Sam. They've missed me from the farmyard, and if they see this odd-looking egg under me, they'll take it. I've done my best and the egg is warm. Take it home and hatch it yourself, Sam Pig.'

'But I can't sit on an egg,' protested Sam. 'I should break it. None of the Pig family are egg-sitters.'

'You can only try, Sam,' said the hen politely and

firmly. 'You wouldn't break it, for it is hard as iron. Now off you go with your egg and don't bother me any more.'

She stalked away to the poultry yard, and Sam picked up the warm egg. He wrapped it in his sleeve and carried it home.

'How's the egg?' asked Brock. 'Has it hatched out yet? Is it a dragon or a Dodo? Perhaps it's a sea-serpent.'

'Oh Brock,' sighed Sam. 'The hen won't sit any longer, and she told me to hatch it myself. What shall I do?'

'We will wrap the egg in sheep's wool and put it in the corner by the fire. Perhaps the warmth will hatch it. You certainly can't sit on it, Sam. You couldn't keep still for five minutes, let alone a week.'

They wrapped the egg in fine wool and put it in a basket on the hearth. For a month it lay there, and the fire never went out. Every morning Sam hurried down to look at his egg, and at last he was rewarded. There was a cheeping sound and a movement in the basket.

'Quick! Come here, everybody! My egg is going to hatch out,' he called, and the little pigs and Brock came running in.

'I believe it will be a crocodile, Sam,' warned Brock. 'Then we shall have to run for our lives, or it will eat us up.'

The egg cracked with a sharp sound like a gun. The pigs leapt back in alarm. A bird with gleaming black and gold feathers came out. Its tail curved with long plumes, it had spurs on its legs, its eyes were gold. It stretched its neck and crowed shrilly.

'Cockadoodle doo!' it cried, and the sound of it went through the air like a high clarion.

'It's a new kind of barndoor cock,' said Sam, and he put out a hand and picked it up.

'Goodness! It isn't soft like an ordinary cock. Brock, it's all hard as iron. Brock!'

Brock took the cock from Sam's arms, and stroked it.

'It's my belief,' he began slowly, 'it's my belief that this is a weather-cock.'

It was true. The cock's feathers were made of iron, tipped with gold and flashing with scarlet. Every little feather was delicate metal, strong and unyielding. The scales on its legs were thin gold and the spurs sharp as needles. The cock stood stiff as the weather-cock on the church steeple.

Brock took it to the door, and it flew with heavy flapping wings to the roof. There it perched, swinging round with the wind. It was strong and stately like the church cock, but it had more life than that iron bird, for every hour it flapped its wings and crowed.

It refused to come down, so Brock made a little weather-vane for it to perch upon. 'North, South, East, West', he marked the vane, and the cock crowed with delight when the Badger fixed it on the gable-end of the house. There it roosted, and there it stayed.

'I suppose it is the son of the weather-cock in the church-yard,' said Sam, 'for that was where I found it.'

'Strange things come out of eggs,' observed Brock, thoughtfully. 'I've heard of many from travellers, but I've never known a weather-cock to be hatched out before.'

'Of course every cock on every church steeple must have been in an egg sometime,' said Ann, looking up at the weather-cock.

'I expect there are lots of weather-cock eggs lying in church-yards, only people don't notice them,' said Bill Pig. 'If we hatched them all we should have cocks on every barn and house-end in the country.'

So up on the gable-end the weather-cock sat, in wind and rain, in storm and sunshine, pointing the direction of the wind. It was a homely happy bird, and when Sam played his fiddle on the doorstep in the evenings, or the little pigs sang in chorus together such rousing songs as 'John Peel', or 'Here's a health unto his Majesty', the weather-cock flapped its wings with delight. It wanted no food, and no water. It drank the dews and rains, and breathed the sweet air. Sometimes Brock climbed up with a bottle of oil and a feather, to grease its iron bones. It might have creaked with rheumatism if he hadn't taken care of it.

There it roosted and there it stayed.

'Cockadoodle doo! It's nine o'clock and a fine night with the wind in the West,' crowed the bird in a high, thin voice, which was sweet and cool as a whistle.

'Cockadoodle doo! It's twelve o'clock and the stars shining, and wind in the North,' it would sing.

The Fox came prowling round with his eyes on the bright eyes of the bird. He wasn't quite sure about it. It was a strange bird to come out of Sam's egg. It might break his teeth if he sprang upon it. He went back to the wood.

'Cockadoodle doo! It's one o'clock and the moon shining,' sang the weather-cock on the house of the four Pigs.

Far away in the church-yard the parent cock heard the cry. 'Cockadoodle doo!' it shrilled in reply, but only the tombstones heard the wheezing bird, for nobody ever gave it any oil.

Sam Pig and the
Little Princess

Did you ever hear how Sam Pig rescued a Princess?
It happened like this. A lovely little Princess lived in
the castle, miles and miles away over the mountains
and woods. She was so beautiful she could turn night
into day, it was said. She was fair as a Madonna lily,
with golden hair like its stamens, and eyes as blue as
the sky above, and she was as good as she was lovely.
She never left the castle gardens, to drive in the town.
She didn't even ride in the Royal Park with the King
and Queen. Very few people had seen her, but they
talked of her exquisite beauty.

Even the birds and butterflies talked about her.
The swallows spoke of her as they perched on the
telegraph wires before their long journeys south.

'We are going to Africa, but we shall not see such
a dainty maid till we return to hawk round the palace
garden,' they said to their children.

The goldfinches twittered in the thistles, and swung
on the prickly stalks. 'Proud Tailors' the children
call the birds. Even Proud Tailors were not as pretty
as the little golden-haired princess.

The wind sang of her, the trees murmured her praise, and all the little breezes begged to be allowed to blow in the castle gardens to see the sweet vision.

Of course the rumour of her charms came at last to the house of the four Pigs.

'Is she as pretty as Sister Ann?' asked Sam Pig.

'I haven't seen her,' replied Brock, 'but the wind says she is far prettier than any creature.'

'Is she prettier than Sister Ann when she wears the locket and chain you gave her for her birthday?' persisted Sam.

'Yes,' growled Brock. 'Don't ask me again. I'm busy.'

Sam was silent, but he very much wanted to see this little girl.

Although the Princess had every grace, there was a drawback which was kept secret. She was light as a feather. When she went into the garden she had to be tied to two stout ladies-in-waiting. Two golden cords bound her to their ample waists. The little Princess didn't like this at all, but it wasn't safe for her to wander alone in the open air. In the castle the windows of her room were kept shut, and the cords were removed from her guardians, but as soon as she stepped into the fresh air and sunshine she had to be tied again. The King and Queen were very much troubled about this defect in their darling, but although they asked the advice of all the famous doctors, nothing could be done to keep her from floating away.

One day the young girl sat among the flowers, reading her fairy book. Her thin gold crown was on her head, her delicate frock of white and silver lace was spread out. The two ladies sat with her. The gold cords holding the three together glistened in the sunshine. The Princess glanced with disgust at the fine gold ropes which held her to the fat ladies-in-waiting. Then she turned the pages of her book. In her pocket was a needlecase with a pair of sharp scissors. She had only to wait.

The sun was hot, the ladies nodded, and nodded again. They fell asleep. The sentries marched up and down. The little dogs frisked on the lawn. Quick as a flash the Princess drew the needlecase from her pocket, and cut the cords with the scissors.

Dancing, leaping, she sprang to her feet, and like a fairy she fluttered, her lace skirts outspread like flower petals, her little feet in their scarlet slippers tripping like butterflies among the flowers.

The sentries looked at her and hesitated. Before they could do anything a sudden wind blew down from the sky. Oh! How it blew! It lifted the little Princess high in the air, and carried her away!

Away she went, clutching the fairy book with one hand and the gold crown with the other. Away! Across the park the wind swept her, where the King and Queen were riding.

The King saw his darling floating like a dandelion seed, and he sent for horses and men to follow. Over the country they sped, seeking the little Princess.

Now that afternoon Sam Pig was walking in the fields near the river, looking for mushrooms. He had a little basket on his arm, and he kept stooping and gathering the satin-coated mushrooms.

'One for me, and one for Brock and one for Ann,' said he, to himself. 'Another for Brock. I shan't give one to Bill or Tom. They don't deserve it.'

Something white floated in the air, hovering like a large butterfly, shining with silver and gold.

'A fine monstrous mushroom come from the sky,' said Sam, and he ran after it. Down into the river dropped the fluttering mushroom, and Sam Pig ran to the water's edge.

'Save me! Save me!' cried a small voice.

'Mushrooms talking,' muttered Sam.

'Save me!' cried the voice again, and two white arms were held up. The wind blew, but the waters held tightly to the girl's skirts. She would have been dragged under the waves down among the fishes and whirlpools, but brave Sam Pig plunged in after her. He seized her slim body and paddled with her ashore. Panting, spluttering, splashing, he paddled with her, and he dragged her up the bank and laid her on the grass. Her silver and white dress was smirched with weeds. Her golden hair was lank and streaming with water. Her face was pale, her eyes closed.

Sam wiped the water from her forehead with his grimy handkerchief, and gently touched her closed eyes. He stroked her wet gold hair, and held the tiny cold fingers.

'A kind of water-maiden,' he murmured. 'Perhaps an air-maiden. Yes, she's an air-maiden, come from the clouds. I'll take her home to Brock, poor little thing.'

He lifted her, and cried out in astonishment.

'She's light as thistledown,' said he. 'Of course that shows she is an air-maiden.'

He carried the little Princess through the meadow. The jolting of Sam, who leapt and ran and danced along his way, must have done the Princess good, for she opened her big blue eyes and stared at the pigling who galloped along with her in his arms.

'Where am I?' she asked, faintly.

'Going home with Sam Pig to see Brock the Badger and Ann and Bill and Tom,' said Sam quickly. 'You be quiet, for you've been nearly drowned.'

She was silent, and Sam bore her through the woods and up the garden to the house of the four Pigs.

'What's this?' asked Brock, as Sam dumped the lovely maiden on to the Badger's chair.

'It's an air-maid,' said Sam. 'Dropped from the clouds, and picked up by Sam Pig at your service.'

'You're a knight-errant,' said Bill with sarcasm.

Brock busied himself looking after the half-drowned child.

'Put her in a warm bath, Ann, and then dress her in your Sunday frock. She's cold as ice, and shivering with fright.'

While Ann got the bath ready, Brock poured out a cordial of herbs, and gave it to the little girl.

'Sup this, my pretty dear,' said he softly, and his voice was so warm and kind that a faint smile came to the girl's pale lips.

'Agrimony, Heart's-ease,
  Put your little heart at ease.
  Saint Peter's Herb and Marygold,
  Cure this little maid of cold,'

chanted Brock.

As she drank the colour came back to her white
cheeks, the rose to her lips. She stopped shivering and
began to laugh at old Brock the Badger.

Then Ann took off the soaking silver and white
dress, and bathed the little girl, and dressed her anew
in a scarlet woollen skirt and bodice, thick and
clumsy.

'She's too light,' complained Ann. 'She floated
in the bath. She must be made of air, Brock.'

'I'm a Princess,' said the child. 'I was blown
away.'

'There now, Brock,' said Sam. 'She's a Princess.
Can we keep her?'

'We'll see,' said Brock.

The little Pigs danced round the chair where the
Princess sat, and Sam played a tune to her on his
fiddle. Tom made a bowl of bread and milk for her,
and Ann filled a sack with new straw and put it in
the bedroom next to her own truckle bed.

'A little sister for Ann.' Tom called the Princess.

Brock, who hung out the silver and white clothes
to dry on the bushes, spied a crown woven on each
garment. Perhaps she was really a Princess. She might
even be the beautiful creature whom they had heard

about. He walked the fields and brought home some things he found in the grass, a thin gold circlet, and a fairy book. He sat up late that night, while the little Princess slept, making a magical cure for her.

The Princess ate the rough fare, and slept on the coarse straw bed. She washed in the running stream, and combed her hair by the water-side. Brock's magic medicine cured her from her feather-lightness, and she found to her joy she could go out on a windy day without being swept off her feet. She could run and leap, with no fear of floating like a cloud in the air.

'My Princess,' Sam called her, and he took her to secret places in the fields where rare flowers bloom, he showed her birds and butterflies, and taught her all he knew of the life of the woods. Everything Brock the Badger had told him he taught his little companion.

The little Princess became brown as a berry, strong as a young colt, and her eyes were trained to see many things of the earth. She was happy, too, always singing and gay, but one day Brock found her in tears.

'What's the matter, child?' he asked kindly.

'I miss my mother. I want her,' said the girl.

'Yes, you ought to have a mother to cosset and pet you,' agreed Brock, 'but we don't know where she is. I'll take you to Farmer Greensleeves' farm. The farmer has a little daughter, and Mrs Greensleeves will mother you. You'll get along famously there. There's plenty of honey and milk and sweet home-made bread.'

Off they went that day, Sam Pig and Brock with the little Princess between them. Brock carried her needlecase and gold scissors, and various articles in his knapsack, wrapped in green leaves. Sam carried the fairy book of the little Princess.

Up the cart road to the farm they walked, Brock in his old clothes like a tramp, Sam in his torn plaid trousers, and the little Princess in her silver and white dress, washed and ironed by Ann, with her silver sash flashing in the sun and her bright hair streaming from her little cap of blossoms. On her shoulders she wore a cloak of leaves and flowers that Ann had sewn to keep her warm on the way. On her feet she had a queer pair of slippers, made out of birch-bark. Her own delicate shoes were no use for walking in farm-land, in mud and water.

Sam led the way through the orchard to the back door of the farm. Softly they stepped down the flagged path among the ferns and rose trees, but the little Princess walked even more quietly than they, for she had learned their ways. They all hid in the lavender bushes, crouching among the spiky flowers, till the back door opened and Farmer Greensleeves himself came out.

'Milking-time,' he shouted. 'Milking-time! Call up the cows! Coo-up! Coo-up!'

Out from the bushes stepped Sam Pig, Brock the Badger, and the little Princess.

'What's this! What be ye?' he cried in bewilderment. 'It's little Sam Pig and Brock the Badger, but who's this girl with ye?'

'Please Master, she's a Princess,' cried Sam, shrilly.

'Farmer Greensleeves,' said Brock, in his best Sunday voice. 'We've brought this little lost maid to stay with you till somebody fetches her. Our cottage is no place for a Princess. We live too rough. You live in a palace, you have cream and honey and new-laid eggs every day. You have a little daughter, and a wife to look after the girl. She will be more settled with you.'

'Where's she from, Brock? My goodness! She is a pretty picture,' said the farmer.

'She just floated down from the sky one day,' said Sam eagerly, 'and I fished her out of the river. She may be an air-maiden, and she may be a kind of water-maid without a tail.'

'Floated down, did she?' said the farmer, stroking his chin thoughtfully.

'I'm a Princess,' said the little girl, in a high clear voice.

'You are, are you?' said the farmer. 'Well, come along in and see the Missis and childer. They'll take care of you, and welcome. I'll put an advertisement in the local paper, and see if a Princess has been lost.'

Out stepped Sam Pig, Brock the Badger, and the little
Princess.

'Blown away,' said the little girl.

'Blown away,' said the farmer.

'Here's her crown,' said Brock, unpacking his knapsack and taking the slender gold circlet from the leaves. We found it in the field. She must have dropped it.'

'Real gold seemingly,' mused the farmer, taking it in his great hand and tapping it.

'Here are her shoes,' added Brock, and he gave the farmer the little shoes of scarlet leather stamped with gold lilies of the crown.

'Like a fairy's,' cried the farmer.

'And here's her pieces of gold cord, we found tied to her waist,' went on Brock, and the farmer stored them in his pocket.

'And here's her fairy book I found in the hedge,' said Sam, and he held out the leather-backed book with every picture painted and enamelled in colours rare. 'Well! Well!' exclaimed the farmer. 'Come along in, all of you, and meet the family.'

'No, thank you,' said Brock. 'We must go home.'

So Brock and little Sam kissed the hand of the little Princess, and turned sadly away down the back path, among lavender and ferns. The girl ran lightly into the kitchen and flung her arms round the astonished farmer's wife.

'A little maid come to visit us,' said Farmer Greensleeves. 'Here are her things. She's a bit upper in life than us. Will you help me to write a good advertisement for the paper, for she's somebody's lost darling?'

'Never did I set eyes on such loveliness,' cried Mrs Greensleeves, holding up her hands in amazement. 'And her clothes! They've got a crown on them! Where has she come from?'

'Out of the clouds, seemingly,' said the farmer.

'Oh, mother, is she an angel?' asked little Mary Greensleeves, but the girl laughed with merry laughter.

'I'm only a Princess,' said she.

'Let's go and see the calves suckled, and then we'll go to the milking and take our china mugs for drinks of new milk,' whispered Mary, and the little Princess clapped her hands.

So out they went to the farmyard, and the little Princess was happy as the day is long. She slept in Mary's room in a white bed with clean lavender-scented linen sheets under a quilt of patchwork. She ate her breakfast in the farm kitchen, and she wore Mary's print dresses by day and her cotton night-gowns by night. She swung in the great oak tree and climbed the apple trees and rode on the grey pony. It was great fun for all.

A month passed, and there was a thunder of hoofs in the yard, and messengers rode up, asking about the little lost girl who had been advertised in the penny paper. They had come from the King himself.

She was his daughter, blown away in a gale, carried light as a feather over the mountains far away.

'She's no feather now,' said Mrs Greensleeves, as she dressed the Princess in the white and silver lace frock, and put the gold crown on her head and the scarlet shoes on her tiny feet.

'I was cured by Brock the Badger,' explained the Princess.

'Then Brock the Badger must have this bag of gold,' said the messenger.

'But little Sam Pig saved me from drowning,' added the Princess quickly.

'Then Mister Brock and Mister Sam Pig must share the bag of gold,' said the man. 'And you, Farmer Greensleeves, must have this purse of gold for your trouble.'

'Nay, we want nothing. The little maid was no trouble at all,' said the farmer, shaking his head.

'Take it! And here is the bag for the two gentlemen, Mister Brock and Mister Pig. Will you give it to them?'

'Certainly. Mister Brock and Mister Pig. Ha! Ha!' laughed the farmer, his sides shaking.

Away rode the messengers, with the Princess sitting behind the captain of the guard. She had no gold cord to hold her; she was free. She waved her little hand, she tossed her golden head, and the glittering company trotted down the lane among the sheep and lambs, between rose-covered hedges.

'Has she really gone?' whispered Sam Pig, creeping out of the lavender bushes. 'Oh, I do miss her! I loved her!'

'Here's a bag of gold for you and Brock,' said the farmer.

'We don't want gold,' sighed Sam. 'Our hearts are broken. Gold won't cure us. Keep it yourself and buy a plough, Farmer Greensleeves.'

'What would you like, Sam? You must have a reward,' said the farmer.

'Just a sack of green apples,' said Sam. 'I think they would cure my heart-ache.'

'They'll maybe give you an ache somewhere else,' laughed the farmer. 'I'll leave a few sacks of apples by the hedge, and you can help yourself. Good-bye, Sam, and thank you for that gold. I can do with it really. Now I can get the barn mended and new thatch on the cart-shed, and new stalls in the cowhouse, as well as a plough and chain-harrow. Thank you, Sam.'

'Good-bye,' said Sam, and he ran back to the cottage to tell of the last glimpse of the little Princess riding away to the palace over the mountains.

Sam Pig and the Brownie

One fine day Sam Pig went to the farm, just to see how everybody was. He climbed on the wall of the pig-cote and chatted to the little pigs. He threw a handful of maize to the hens when nobody was looking. He patted Sally the Mare and gave her a message from Brock. He milked Rosie the Red Cow as she stood in the field and he sipped the sweet frothing milk from the little can. Nobody saw him, he was so nimble and spry, and even if they had seen a small fat pig in check trousers wandering about the farm, it wouldn't have surprised them. Since Sam had worked in the hayfield and gone to market with Farmer Greensleeves he had been accepted as a friend. Sam never counted on this friendship; he came and went like a shadow, disturbing nobody, avoiding the family, and talking only to his familiars, the farm animals.

On this day he was starting off home again, with an egg that the brown hen had given him in his pocket, and a rhubarb leaf under his hat for coolness, when he heard clack, clack, clack. He turned aside down

the little cool paved path among the ferns which led
to the dairy door. There, with her wooden churn
near the water trough stood Mollie the dairymaid,
making the butter. She turned the handle and the
wooden perforated splasher inside the churn sent
the cream against the smooth walls with a sound like
the flapping of slippers. Slap, slap, slap went the
cream, and the handle clacked as it turned. Sam
crouched in a lavender bush and waited for the
butter to come.

It was a hot day, and the scent of the lavender and
the smell of milk drifted in waves around little Sam.
The music of the clacking churn, the tinkle of water
in the stone trough, and the song of the cuckoo made
a lullaby for Sam Pig. He nearly fell asleep. Then
Mollie began to sing her own butter-making song,
like this:

> 'Come butter, come,
> Come butter, come,
> Peter Paul, let it fall,
> Come butter, come.'

But the butter didn't come, and poor Mollie got quite
red in the face as she turned the churn. She opened
the lid and peered inside, muttering 'Is anybody
there? Are you playing your tricksies, little Goblin?
Are you there, Robin?'

Sam thought he heard a faint chuckle, a peal of
bell-like laughter, but Mollie shook her head and

latched the lid again. She went on churning, singing her butter song. For an hour she worked, and at last the noise of the dasher changed. Soft thuds and little thumps told of the newly-formed balls of butter beating the sides of the churn.

'Butter's coming! It's coming at last! It's never been so long. I'm sure there's been you-know-who playing tricksies on me,' she cried, running indoors to tell her mistress. Sam Pig scrambled out of the bushes. He was stiff with hiding there. There is a little airhole in the side of a churn, and from it poked a little round head. Then a wee body wriggled through and the small figure of a man came tumbling down the churn, leaping and dancing over the stones, turning cart-wheels with no sound at all.

Sam stretched out a hand and caught him.

'Let me go! Let me go!' shrieked the tiny creature, kicking and biting Sam's hand, but Sam didn't care about that. He held tightly to the manikin, and stuffed him in his wide pocket.

'I didn't do any harm,' cried the little person, in a muffled voice.

'Who are you? What were you doing in Mollie's churn?' asked Sam.

'I'm only a little Goblin. I belong to Mister Green-sleeves' Farm. I was teasing Moll because she forgot my bowl of milk. Besides, she has no right to call me Robin,' said the Goblin, sulkily. 'Let me go.'

'No. I don't catch a little Goblin every day,' said Sam. 'You're coming home with me. We haven't got a Goblin at our house.'

'I'll give you a purse of gold,' said the tiny voice from the pocket.

'Don't want it,' said Sam. 'What's the use of gold to a family of four Pigs and Brock the Badger?'

'Four Pigs and Brock the Badger,' echoed the little Goblin, surprised, and then he was silent. He didn't speak till Sam brought him out of his pocket and set him on the kitchen table, keeping a tight hold of his body lest he should escape.

'Look what came out of the butter churn,' cried Sam, proudly displaying his catch.

The little man bowed and nodded to the astonished pigs.

'I've not come here of my own free will,' he explained. 'I belong to Farmer Greensleeves's farm. You'd best send me back. The farm and I belong to each other. I'm a hard-working respectable little Goblin, I am. They can't do without me. I belong there.'

'You can't belong there,' scoffed Bill. 'Farmer Greensleeves wouldn't have you. You're too little to do any work. How could an elf like you plough or milk or harrow or reap?'

'I belong to Woodseats Farm, not to the farmer,' insisted the Goblin. 'I have lived there for nigh on three hundred years and guarded the place from harm. Only once did I leave. That was when lazy Farmer Hobbs lived at the farm. It was in the reign of Queen Anne.'

'Queen Anne! Queen Anne!' cried little Ann Pig. 'Who was Queen Anne?' But nobody could tell her.

The door was pushed open and Brock the Badger entered.

'Hello!' cried he. 'Isn't this the Brownie from Woodseats Farm? I've seen you whisking into holes, peeping from kettles and pots. What are you doing away from home?'

'Your friend, Sam Pig, brought me against my will, stuffed in his pocket.' The Goblin frowned at Sam and shook his tiny fist at him.

'He was spoiling the butter,' said Sam.

'Sam!' said Brock sternly.

'It's true,' went on the Goblin. 'I did it to teach Moll a lesson. She called me by my secret name, Robin. I won't be talked about. I am a secret one, not to be mentioned.'

'Never mind, little Goblin. Never mind,' said Brock soothingly.

'Stay with us, little Goblin,' invited Ann Pig, shyly. 'We have herb broth and pease pudding, and frittery treacle pancakes for supper.'

'And you shall have my silver spoon to sup with,' said Sam. 'I am sorry, Goblin, that I was rude to you.'

'You shall drink from the mug I carved out of a

Sam brought him out of his pocket and set him on the
kitchen table.

nut-shell for the Leprechaun who once visited us,' said Tom.

'And wear his leather shoe if you wish,' added Bill.

The Goblin smiled and leapt lightly down from the table. 'Thank you kindly, good folk. I shall be glad to sup with you. As for the Leprechaun, that Irish sprite, I have no truck with him.'

'Can you do magics like the Leprechaun?' asked Ann Pig later, when they all sat round the table, the little Brownie perched on a log that Brock had put for him.

'Magic? Yes if I wish, but I don't wish,' replied the little man, supping the broth with Sam's silver saltspoon. 'We Brownies guard ancient houses and keep them from harm. If a Brownie lives in a house that is indeed good fortune for the householder. We reward the good and punish the evil doers. Once at the farm there was a bad stable boy, and he neglected the horses. I nipped him and put sour dreams in his mind. He soon changed his ways. Now there is old Adam, and he cares for Sally the Mare. I sweep the stable for him and sit in Sally's manger at nights if she is lonely. I comb her mane and plait her tail and fettle her right well.'

'What else do you do, Brownie?' asked Ann, helping the Goblin to more soup.

'I clean the kitchen at nights when the family is abed. I polish the boots, and tidy the cinders, and sweep the crumbs. There's a little besom behind the door all ready for me. I scour the pans in the dairy, and wipe the eggs when I'm in a good humour and everybody has been laughing and kind. When they are bad-tempered I let them do their work themselves.'

'Do you never sleep, Brownie?' asked Sam.

'Oh yes, I sleep for a few hours, curled up with the cat on the hearth.'

'Stay the night with us, dear Lob-lie-by-the-fire,' persuaded Brock. 'We have never had a Brownie in our house.'

'Yes, stay, dear Brownie,' implored the others.

'Well, I may, but I ought not to leave the farm. I'm its protector. Still, I expect it will be all right for once,' said the Brownie, hesitating and smiling.

That evening was a merry time, for the little pigs played games with the Brownie. He taught them ancient games he had played in far away days, when Queen Elizabeth was on the throne, and his brothers and relations lived in every old house in the land of England.

He taught them Nine Men's Morris, and Tippit Tappit, which they played on the floor with a stick and wedge of wood. They taught the Brownie Hop-Scotch, and Ann drew little squares with chalk on the stone flags for them to hop into. The Goblin out-hopped them all, and won every game easily. Even when they played nine-pins with the little wooden men Brock had made, he bowled every nine-pin over with one ball.

Then Brock told a tale of a dancing bear he once saw which escaped at night from the inn and came to the woods. The Goblin told of the days when a Royalist fugitive had hidden at the farm. Soldiers hunted for him in barn and stable and kitchen, but they never found him.

'Where was he?' asked Sam.

'I took him to a secret hiding-place in the thick walls, which is still there. There are no Royalist fugitives now, but if the time comes and enemies are near, I shall be ready.'

So they chattered and at last it was time to go to bed. The Goblin lay down by the fire, and Sam begged to sleep by the Brownie's side. Brock also stayed downstairs, sleeping in his arm-chair as he often did. He was wakeful at night, and sometimes he went out to prowl among the hills, to visit the Otter far away on the moor, or to wander in the woods, breathing the rich, exciting scents of darkness and dawn. Brock sat in his chair, and Sam Pig and the little Brownie curled near him by the dying embers.

After a time the Brownie sprang to his feet, head raised as if he were listening to a distant sound. Then down to the earth he dropped, with his pointed ear pressed to the stones. Brock also rose and little Sam Pig jumped up in a quiver of excitement.

'What is there? I hear nothing,' said Brock.

'There is danger at the farm tonight. I must go. I ought not to have left my post. Something is wrong,' muttered the little Goblin man.

'I'll come with you,' said Brock, quietly taking his cudgel and opening the door.

'And I too,' said little Sam Pig.

Into the black night the three stepped, and away they went, Brock running with his fast steady trot, Sam padding after, and the Goblin leaping like a hare, so fast that the others could hardly keep pace with him. Brock was making for the farmhouse, but the Brownie turned towards the stable. He glanced through the keyhole, and saw that all was well. Then he darted to the stackyard. Brock and Sam silently followed, their eyes gleaming, their senses alert. They knew that somebody was about on evil errand. Two shadows moved across the golden stacks, with little flickers of flame in their hands.

'Stack-firers!' whispered the Brownie. 'You tackle them, Brock and Sam Pig, while I rouse the farmer and the farm hands. Quick. Fire is dangerous, for there is no water. Stacks flare up in a moment.'

Off he went, and Brock dropped on all fours, bared his splendid teeth, and charged the men. They were tall and strong, and he was only a small animal. They had clubs and sticks, but Badger's great chance was the surprise of the attack. He was on them before they saw him. They tried to beat him off, and plunged the burning wisps of hay in his face. Sam Pig charged them with his hard head and his little fighting fists. He was like a wild cat, as he bit and tore.

'It's a Badger,' shouted one of the men. 'It's a wild Badger at us, and something else. There's another!'

Brock got his teeth into the leg of the first man, and the second laid about him with the cudgel, beating Brock's head till the blood flowed. Round and round leapt little Sam Pig, helping Brock, and Brock held tight to his man. A flickering fire was licking up the sides of the great stacks of hay, and if it got well alight the flames would spread to all the three great stacks, which Farmer Greensleeves had laboured to make for the winter's supply. From them the fire would reach the barns and stable, and the old house itself.

In the meantime the little Goblin raced to the house, through the tiny gap in the door, which was his own doorway, upstairs to the farmer's chamber. He squeezed through the thumb-hole above the latch, and climbed on the farmer's bed. Farmer Greensleeves lay snoring with the clothes drawn up round his head. The little Goblin pulled the blankets away and whispered urgently into his ear.

'Master! Master! Fire! Fire! Fire!'

That was enough. That word, 'Fire', was the one word the farmer dreaded. He would have wakened from the dead if somebody said 'Fire' to him, he once said. He opened his eyes, sprang from the bed

The Goblin, leaping like a hare, so fast that the others could
hardly keep pace with him.

wide awake in a moment. He roused his wife, and rang the alarm bell for the servant men. Then out he went to the stackyard, his gun in his hand. A fire meant foul play. He heard the cries and muffled chokes of the men whom Brock and Sam Pig held, and he saw thin flames running over the stack.

He fired his gun as he ran. The men lay on the ground, with dark animals near. Brock and Sam Pig let go and slipped into the shadows to watch. The farm men came running up with pitchforks.

'Here they are! One of them's the stable lad I sent away. Take them and shut them up under lock and key. Then make a chain of water for the fire. It's only just started; it hasn't got a hold yet. We shall put it out.'

So they formed a living chain and passed water along, from the pond, and beat out the fire with brushes. In a few minutes all was over and the hay and farm saved.

'How did you find out, Master? Did you see or hear 'owt?' asked old Adam.

'No,' said Farmer Greensleeves, wiping the sweat from his face. 'No. I was fast asleep, and I dreamed 'Fire. Fire'. Just like that. I heard a voice calling in my dreams. So up I got and I knew there was a fire.'

'Dreams is powerful things. They's sent as warnings. Some says the little people warn us, and there's one about this farm, Master, as you doubtless know.'

The farmer nodded, and made a sign for silence. Brownies don't like to be spoken about.

'But who held those men? That's what I want to know,' he added. 'That wasn't one of *them*. There were two animals, I just got a glimpse, and not our Rover either, for he's chained up.'

'It was a Badger, and somebody like a Pig,' said the man when they questioned him. 'It was a savage Badger out of the woods, and a savage young Pig maybe.'

'A Badger and a Pig.' The farmer gave a sudden

laugh and went off to the house. The police were on the way, and the men were caught and the stacks were saved. He had something to be thankful for.

Badger and Sam ran light-footed home, dirty and bleeding and happy. As they bathed in the tin tub and put Brock's ointment on their wounds, they told the awakened family about their adventure.

'If the little Brownie hadn't gone back, the farm and all the cowhouses, barns, stables might have been destroyed,' said Brock. 'He saved them, for that is his work on earth. He is the guardian of that old farm, the spirit of old watching over it.'

'I wish we had a Brownie to look after us,' said Tom Pig.

'We don't need no Brownie, Goblin, Lob-lie-by-the-fire,' said Sam loyally. 'We've got old Brock the Badger. He takes care of us and guards our little house.'

'I do my best,' said Brock humbly. 'I do my best, that is when you let me.'

Away at the farm Mrs Greensleeves was talking to her dairymaid. 'It's my belief it was the Brownie who warned us,' she whispered. 'We'll put a little pat of butter with his bowl of milk on the dairy floor, and mind you don't call him Robin or Hob, for he doesn't like it.'

'All right, Missis,' said Mollie the dairymaid, and she took her candle and went back to bed.

Sam Pig and the Penny

Brock gave Sam Pig a new penny for his Mid-summer Day present. It was a beautiful penny, fresh from the mint. It shone bright as the sun in the sky, and the picture of King George was clear as the man in the moon. An old lady had given the coin to Brock, mistaking him for a tramp as he slouched along the lane one dusky night.

'Take this, my poor man, and buy yourself some-thing to eat,' said she, fumbling in her purse. Badger nearly choked with indignation, but he was flattered at his guise being accepted so readily. He kept the new penny till Midsummer Day, which is a day of rejoicing in the wide world of field and wood, and he gave it to Sam Pig.

Sam was delighted at the gift. He showed it to all his friends and neighbours. The Fox looked at it with envy. He said there was something magical about it, and he warned Sam against keeping it. Sally the Mare said she had seen Farmer Greensleeves bring a bagful of new pennies from the bank. Sam hunted in the grassy banks among the daisies and forget-me-nots, but he couldn't find another penny – let alone a bagful.

It was certainly a precious coin, but alas! it fell through a hole in Sam's pocket. He heard it rattle on the stones and then he saw it rolling away. Of course he stooped to pick it up, but the penny darted off. It bowled merrily down the lane on its rim and Sam Pig trotted after it with a hand outstretched to catch it.

'Stop! Stop!' cried Sam Pig, but the penny rolled away. It wouldn't wait for little Sam. It had a desire to escape from the darkness of a pocket. It wanted to see life, to peep at the green world where the sun shone and the birds sang.

So away it went, the bold little adventurer, twinkling like gold in the sunlight. After it ran Sam Pig, and his little legs twinkled too, he ran so fast. The penny bounced over the stones, it leapt across the ruts and sprang over the ditches. It fairly danced down the lane, swerving sometimes to the right, sometimes to the left to avoid Sam Pig. Sam stooped over it as he hurried, but the penny always managed to leap aside from his clutch.

The lane joined the road, and there the penny went swifter, for the way was smoother. It bowled along like a wheel, and as it moved it began to sing in a low coppery voice like the hum of a bumble bee:

'You cannot catch me,
I'm off for a ramble,
Through fields and lane,
O'er brier and bramble.'

It darted through the hedge into the field and Sam Pig scrambled after. Back it came, bouncing and hopping through the blackberry bushes, as if it had at least half a dozen legs, and Sam followed.

Along the road came Sally the Mare. She had cast a shoe, and she was going to the blacksmith's for a new one. They were busy at the farm so she was going to the village by herself.

'Art thou sure thou canst manage alone?' asked the farmer.

Sally nodded her great shaggy head. So off she went with the money for the shoeing tied in a little bag to her halter. When she saw Sam Pig stooping and running and stooping again, dodging here and there as if he were chasing a butterfly, she cantered to catch him up.

'Hello, Sam. Where are you going so fast and so crookedly?' she asked.

'I'm trying to catch my runaway penny,' panted Sam.

'I'll go with you,' said Sally, and she trotted behind little Sam, not very fast, because her shoe was missing.

'Stop, penny. Wait a moment, penny,' shouted Sam, but the penny seemed to kick up its heels and leap like a hare over the sticks and stones, through the dock leaves and nettles by the roadside, under violets and round the green cowls of the Lords and Ladies.

As Sally the Mare jogged along the bag of money got loose and out leapt a penny. It rolled swiftly ahead and joined the bright new penny belonging to Sam. It was a Queen Victoria penny, battered and dark, but the King George penny could see that its heart was good. Together they ran, rolling cheerfully in company, talking as they went.

'Will you marry me?' asked the bright new penny of King George.

'Indeed I will,' answered the penny of Queen Victoria.

They began to sing a charming duet:

> 'You cannot catch us,
> We are coins of the crown,
> We are going to be married
> When we get to town.'

They jingled their heads together, and jangled their tails, and laughed with tinkling laughter as Sam Pig and Sally the Mare came running after. Of course Sam was getting tired and the mare had only three shoes, but those pennies had something magical about them to spin along so quickly. Perhaps it was love that makes the world go round and spins the pennies along the high-roads of the world.

> 'Where shall we marry?'
> Asked the penny, King George.
> Victoria answered,
> 'At the smith's forge.'

Away they went, rolling through the silver daisies, the freckled cowslips, the pale primroses at the road-side, startling the ants and bees and scarlet-coated ladybirds.

'Penny is a brave coin,
Penny is a Queen.
She shall be married
On the village green.

Penny is a fine coin,
Penny is a King.
He shall be married
With an iron ring,'

they chanted, humming like a hive of bees as they
ran.

Along the road they trundled, the two pennies
prancing and hopping, Sam Pig and the grey mare
plodding after. They came to the river, with its
sparkling water and dipping willows. The pennies
rolled across the bridge and Sam Pig and the mare
trotted after.

Downhill and uphill, across flowery meadows, and
under hedges of may blossom, by clear streams, and
over reedy ditches they went, the two pennies in
front, Sam and the mare not far behind, but never
near enough to catch the runaways.

They passed through a herd of cattle and Rosie
the Red Heifer came running to her friend Sam Pig.

'What's the matter, Sam? Why are you running so
fast?' she asked, mooing gently as she ran alongside
Sam.

'Oh, come and help us, Rosie. My penny is
running away with Sally's penny and we can't catch
them.'

On they went, the gentle red heifer, the old mare and Sam
Pig, and the two pennies trundled in front side by side.

So out from the field leapt the red heifer. She put down her horns and tried to toss the rolling pence, but they slipped away and laughed with shrill cries, and sang their song close to her snuffling nostrils.

'You cannot catch us,
We are coins of King George.
We shall be wed
At the blacksmith's forge.'

'Did you hear that, Sally?' asked Sam. 'They are going to be married at the blacksmith's. How can they?'

'The smith marries runaway couples over the anvil, so I have heard,' said Sally. 'I don't think he will bother to marry two pennies. He will pop them in his leather pocket and spend them at the inn. He won't marry them.'

On they went, the gentle red heifer, the old mare and Sam Pig, and the two pennies trundled in front side by side.

Rover the farm dog joined them.

'Why are you running so fast, little Sam Pig, and Rosie and Sally?' he asked.

'We are trying to catch the two runaway pennies,' said Sam. 'Do come and help us.' So with them ran Rover, his mouth open, his tongue lolling, his jaws ready to snap up the pennies, if only they had stopped a moment. But they didn't. Sam thought he saw two tiny arms outstretched from one to another.

He saw their faces smile, and their eyes blink. They looked very happy, racing to the blacksmith's forge to be wed.

From the pond flew a lily-white Duck, and she too joined in the chase. Then from out of the wood stepped the Fox, his long nose sniffing, his sharp eyes on the Duck.

'What's the matter, Sam Pig? Why are you running so fast, with Sally the Mare, and Rosie and Rover and the white lady Duck?'

'Oh, we're trying to catch the runaway pennies, who are off to be married at the blacksmith's forge,' panted Sam wearily.

'I'll come with you and help you,' said the Fox, and he joined the company.

Now when the Duck heard the Fox's feet padding behind her, she took to her wings and flew over the pennies. Her shadow startled them, and they swerved aside. The Fox snapped at the Duck, Rover took a bite at the Fox, Rosie the Heifer tried to toss Rover, and Sally the Mare kicked at the Cow. They rushed away in confusion, back to the pond, the wood, the fields, all except Sally the Mare and little Sam Pig, who followed the pennies down the narrow side-lane.

Up a garden path and through an open door went the pennies, humming and singing their song. Through the kitchen and out at the back door they rolled, and little Sam scuttled after, but Sally went round about the garden.

'Mercy me! What's going on this morning? What's to do?' cried Miss Tabitha Todd, dropping her knitting and leaping on a chair out of the way.

Already Sam and the pennies were in the lane, and Sally came clumping round the corner. They rolled across the village market-place, and a cloud of white dust followed them, with Sam Pig and Sally the Mare.

The pennies ran under the petticoats of Widow Waley, and the poor Widow screamed for she thought they were mice.

They darted close to Farmer Barley, and he tried to plant his foot upon them.

Lawyer Limb reached for his spectacles and peered uneasily at the ground.

Policeman Bunting took out his pocket-book and wetted his pencil and wrote very slowly, 'Two pence, running wild.'

At the other side of the market-square was the smithy, and into the wide door ran the pennies. The great fire burned in the corner, and the boy was blowing it with the bellows. The smith took a red-hot horse-shoe from the fire and beat it on the anvil. He raised his mighty arms to strike it again. The two pennies leapt high in the air, and sprang on the shoe lying there.

'Clang!' went the hammer. 'Tinkle, tinkle!' cried the pennies, and in a moment they were married. They had become part of the horse-shoe, one with the iron.

Sally the Mare walked sedately into the smithy.

She was tired of racing after the runaways, and her foot ached.

'Hello, Sally. A shoe missing? Come along. I'm ready for you. Here's a shoe, and I'll fit you.'

So the smith shod Sally with the shoe that had two pennies in it, and Sam Pig leaned on the doorpost watching.

'There's a penny missing, Sally,' said the smith, counting the money, but the mare shrugged her great shoulders and ambled out.

Sam Pig walked home behind Sally. His head drooped wearily, his legs were stiff. He had lost his penny, he was tired and dusty and cross. He heard little voices coming from the horse-shoe, singing, 'We're married! We're married!'

He sang back to them the old song.

> 'Now you're married, you must obey,
> You must be true in all you say.
> You must be kind, you must be good,
> And help your wife to chop the wood.'

The only reply the two pennies made was this:

> 'We're welded together, we never can part,
> We're the luck of the shoe, the love in its heart.'

As for Sam, he said the next time he got a penny he would bore a hole in it and hang it round his neck, so that it could never run away.

Sam Pig and the Water-maid

Do you remember the water-baby Sam found one day when he was fishing in the river? He never forgot that charming child, whom he carried home in his fishing-net, and often he looked in the deep green waters hoping to see the gold head and fish tail of the water-baby.

One day he sat on the river bank fishing, with his creel by his side and his willow rod baited with a scarlet berry bobbing on the water. Sam gazed at the fishes gliding among the water weeds, turning and darting as they played together. The weeds were dragged by the river like green hair, and the fishes' bodies glinted and gleamed like quick-silver. They were far too happy to be caught by little Sam Pig. Sam sniffed the smell of mud and nettles and garlic flowers, scents of the water-side. They were good smells, and fishing was a good sport.

After a time he began to sing, softly, like the water's own music.

'Come along little fish, come take a bite. Come along, dilly-dilly.'

'We won't dilly-dilly with you. We won't be caught,' sang the fish, dancing on their tails and flicking their transparent fins at Sam.

But one fat little fish ate the berry, and Sam hurled the line through the air and had it in a jiffy. He smoothed the ruffled tail, and spoke soothingly to the agitated fish.

'You're coming home to be fried in our frying-pan. We've got a new frying-pan, and nothing to fry in it. You will like to be the first, won't you?'

'I don't want to be a fried fish. You must set me free, Sam Pig. I am the favourite fish-in-waiting to the youngest water-maid. I keep her gold comb. If you let me go I will let you see it.'

'All right. Show me the comb,' said Sam. 'And you might mention to the water-baby that Sam Pig is here on the bank and would like a glimpse of her. After all, I knew her once.'

He threw the fat little fish into the river, and round and round it circled, panting with joy, wriggling its tail, taking deep gulps of the rich water. Then it dived down and appeared again with a glittering gold comb in its mouth. It swam near the bank so that Sam could see the water-maid's treasure. Even as Sam looked at it, shining green-gold in the water, there was a faint splash and the head of the water-maid appeared. Out of the river she raised herself, and clung to a mossy rock which projected from the water. She shook her long golden hair, and the water-drops fell in a rainbow sparkle. The fish held up the comb, and she combed the straight tresses. Her movements were so smooth and fish-like that Sam could hardly believe his eyes. She seemed part of the ever-changing ripple and shadow and flash of light on the water's surface. Sam crouched on the bank among the tall purple loose-strife, scarcely daring to breathe lest she should melt away into the river of which she was a daughter. A water-vole on the bank watched her, and the swallows dipped to the water close to her head. She went on combing her hair, drying it in the sun and wind, and the flickering river lights chequered her with green and violet.

'Sam Pig is there. Sam Pig is hiding there,' whispered the fish, swimming round the dark rock. The water-maid flashed her eyes at Sam, but she said nothing.

She dipped her white hand in the water and drew from the waves a small golden harp. She played a tune as sweet as the warbling of a brook. Sam's heart beat like a little drum in his breast as he listened to the music and watched the lovely water-maid. Her eyes were green as the spring wheat, her skin white as the tips of the frothing waves as they curled round the rock. She wore a dress of grasses, and her bodice was formed of the silky petals of white water lilies with the gold stamens spangling it like jewels. A crystal-clear stone hung from a thin chain at her slender neck. She was small, slim, a child of the water.

She played a tune as sweet as the warbling of a brook.

It was her face, with its mischievous puckered smile that attracted Sam, and he laughed back when she looked at him.

'Sam Pig,' she called, and her voice was like the water itself, singing always. 'Sam Pig! Where's your fiddle, Sam? Where's your music?' She flicked her silver-green tail on the rock, and shook back her golden mane of hair.

Sam blinked and winked and choked. He couldn't find words to speak to such a wonderful creature. She had changed since she was the small water-baby Sam had carried off. She was like a princess of the river, a small queen of the fishes.

She swept her wet fingers over the harp wires and a ripple of music came through the air. She sang instead of talking and her voice went high and low as she said, 'Where's your fiddle, Sam? How is your Sister Ann? Where is Brock the Badger?'

'They are at home,' answered Sam, climbing so close to the river's edge he nearly fell in.

'Take care, Sam. Take care,' laughed the water-maid. 'Sam, I want to see your family. Sam, take me to them.'

Sam's heart beat wildly. Then he remembered something.

'What about the river? We don't want the river to come after you and drown us. It flowed all about our garden and in at the house the last time you came.'

'Hush!' whispered the water-maid. She slipped silently from the rock and glided through the water to the bank. In a moment she was by Sam's side.

'Hush! I will escape for a while. That would be an adventure. The river won't miss me. It is sleepy today. I do want to see little Ann Pig and Brock and all of you.'

Sam was embarrassed. He wondered how the water-maid would walk across the fields and lanes, for a tail is nothing to walk with. He didn't like to mention this drawback to the water-maid, so he waited, and the green tail flicked gently among the flowers near him.

'Where is your water-road? How can I travel?' asked the girl.

'Water-road? I goes up and down the lanes and fields,' said Sam. 'I goes by solid earthy road, not water-road.'

'Surely there is a stream near your cottage? How do you fill your kettle? How do you bathe your body?' asked the maid.

'I don't wash much,' confessed Sam. 'I'm not partial to bathing. There is a stream goes past our garden right down to the river. That's where I fill the kettle for Ann.'

'I know where it enters,' said the water-maid. 'It is a shallow stream and I have never been up it, but I will swim there and join you, if you wait for me.'

Without a moment's hesitation she was gone, and only a flash of gold and an ever-widening ripple showed where a water-maid had been.

Sam collected his creel and his fishing-rod and mackintosh, and then he ran as fast as his twinkling little legs could carry him over the ditches and across the meadows to the stream. When he reached the field where the stream flowed gently amid drifts of creamy meadowsweet and yellow iris, he saw the water-maid waiting for him. How quickly she had come! She was plucking the iris and binding the amber flowers in a wreath for her hair. She smiled when Sam came panting through the mowing grass with his check trousers flapping and his hat awry.

'Now we will go along together,' said she, 'I on my water-way and you on the grass-way. I love these meadows and this clear stream with the pebbles caught in the sunrays. The river bank is deep, and I seldom see over the land, but here I can watch butterflies and bumble-bees and goldfinches and dippers. Pick me some white orchis, Sam. Get lots of pretty things for me. This is my holiday.'

She flicked her transparent green tail, and paddled quietly up the shallow stream, resting here and there, while Sam ran about the fields gathering all the most precious flowers: the bee orchis, lady's tresses, violet-blue geranium and ice-pink centaury.

Sally the Mare was feeding in a field through which they passed, and she came walking slowly to speak to

Sam. She heard his voice, and another's, a cool singing voice like the tinkle of a harp. Sally was curious, and she snuffed the air, and whinnied.

'Sally, Sally! Come here! Look who's here! The water-baby, growed quite a lot! Look at her!' called Sam to his friend.

The mare ambled up and looked at the water-maid.

'Sally, Sally, Sally,' whispered the water-maid, and she held up her cool white fingers, and the mare bent her head humble before her. The wet fingers stroked the mare's neck, and rubbed the white star on her face.

'Dear Sally,' whispered the water-maid.

Sally was taken aback by the strangeness of the water-maid. She didn't speak. She stood still, trembling as the caressing fingers moved over her skin. Then she gave a little snort and turned away.

'Sally didn't say a word,' said Sam, surprised.

'No, she didn't speak, but I knew her thoughts, and that was enough. She's happy is Sally.'

So the water-maid went on her way, and everywhere there came somebody to look at her in wonder. The cows raised their heads and watched her with their big brown eyes. The little colt galloped near, and then shied away and ran like a rocking-horse, The lambs frisked and played by the water-side, bleating their joy at the sight of the pretty creature.

'There's our cottage,' said Sam, pointing across

the pasture. 'There's our orchard, with Ann's washing hanging out, and you can see our chimney among the crabapple trees.'

'I remember,' laughed the water-maid gleefully. 'We all climbed up those trees to get away from the river, and I dived down into its arms.'

'But you were only a baby,' objected Sam.

'I remember all the same. We water folk never forget even the shapes of clouds which change every moment, or the patterns of sunlight and shade. We remember the sprays of rain and the ripples and whirls on water, and moonshine down below. Everything we see remains with us.'

They reached the point where the stream swung away from the cottage, by the shallows where a spring entered. The water-maid came out of the stream and flipped over the grass by Sam's side. Brock was leaning over the gate. He opened it, and walked towards them, much astonished to see Sam's companion.

'She's the water-maid, Brock,' called Sam. 'She's our water-baby growed up. She's come to see us. Where's our Ann?'

'Welcome, little water-maid,' said Brock politely. 'Let me help you. The stones are rough on our path.'

He picked her up and carried her indoors.

'Oh! Look who's come,' cried Ann, running forward and dropping her rolling-pin. 'Oh, how lovely you are!'

'Dear Ann Pig,' murmured the water-maid in her

musical sing-song voice. She gazed round the kitchen with approval. Yes, there were the rush mats on the clean stone floor, and the bath in the corner and the

framed picture with pressed flowers on the wall. There was the cuckoo clock and Badger's armchair and the shelf where all the treasures lay, and bunches of herbs hanging from the beam in the ceiling.

'My home is quite different,' said she, shaking her gold locks and spraying water over the floor.

'What is it like under the river?' asked Sam.

'My sisters and I live in a cave hollowed out under the river bed, where the water is very deep. The floor is fine sand, like gold, and there is an arched roof, and windows with pillars holding them. No herbs hang from our roof beams, but many coloured fish swim in and out of the windows like swallows. Water weeds drip and sway with the wind. There are pretty shells that belong to the river, our father, and curious stones edge our garden, and jewels rare are hidden below, centuries old.'

Her voice was like running water, her eyes like stars, and her golden hair lay over her shoulders like a cloak. The little pigs were enchanted by their guest. Suddenly one of them remembered.

'Will the river come for you? Will it?' asked Bill in alarm.

'No. I hope not. It was asleep when I crept away, and I shall go back soon.'

'Oh stay!' implored little Sam Pig. 'You mustn't go yet. We have so much to show you. There's the garden, and the farm, and the scarecrow in Farmer Greensleeves' field, and rocks in Dragon Wood.'

'No,' said the water-maid, shaking her head. 'I can't live without water near.' Then she asked Sam Pig to play on his fiddle.

Sam took it from the hook and tuned it and played a fine tune called 'The Irishman's Lament', which the Irish haymakers had taught him.

The water-maid picked up her harp and played to

the little pigs. The music rippled so melodiously from those gold wires that the family wanted her to go on for ever. She ran her fingers over the harp, and the little pigs saw pictures of flowing water, in sun and in storm, they saw strange curving shapes of waves, and the criss-cross patterns of gold made by sunlight falling through eddies.

The water-maid talked of the wonders of water, and the way it moves through and under the earth. She spoke of voles and sand martins, and dippers and all the company of water birds and beasts.

Brock talked of horses and fairs and turkeycocks and dancing bears. The little pigs sat in a circle round the two, listening to the fine conversation.

'Do you know Jack Otter?' interrupted Sam Pig.

'Oh yes! I know him well. He comes down the river and plays round our doorway. Then we sisters play our harps, for all otters love music. He brings us news from the hills.'

'He knows us too,' said Sam. 'Once I went to see him, miles away, where the stream becomes nothing at all in the moors.'

'I couldn't go there,' said the water-maid. 'The water is too shallow for me, but I shall tell Jack Otter I have seen you again.'

She suddenly stopped and help up her white hand for silence. The pigs listened intently and Brock threw wide the door.

'Gr-gr-gr-gr,' came a distant growl of the river, and a cold wind blew in at the door.

'There's a storm rising,' said Tom Pig.

There was a flash of lightning, and a roar of thunder, and big drops of rain spattered down.

'I must go,' said the water-maid. 'The river is awake. It is looking for me. I must go.'

'Would you like an umbrella?' asked Ann, but they all laughed at her.

'No,' said the smiling water-maid. 'I love the rain. I shall move swiftly along the water-lane to the river now.'

She said good-bye to the family, and Brock picked her up in his strong arms and carried her down the garden to the stream. She held her little harp tightly, and clutched a bunch of lavender Ann Pig gathered for her.

'Take this, Ann, in memory of me,' she called, tossing the crystal stone which she wore to Ann.

Then she dropped into the water of the stream. The thunder roared, and the rain poured down, and she tossed her wet hair from her face, as she swam away.

'Gr-gr-gr-gr,' the noise of the river grew louder, and the stream swelled and overflowed its banks.

'Brock and I will go with you to see you safely in the river,' shouted Sam, running alongside.

They raced through the meadows, and the water-maid moved swiftly with no effort through the water.

Louder grew the roar of the river, and wilder the storm.

Sally was sheltering by the wall, and the cattle stood with their backs to the tempest as the water-maid passed by.

At last they saw the river, dashing against its banks, tearing at the roots of trees with foam-tipped fingers, snarling and growling as if in pain. They heard its deep voice demanding the return of the water-maid.

'Where are you, my daughter? Where are you? I am coming to seek you, over meadow and valley. I will drown the world to find you. Oh, my best-loved daughter,' moaned the river.

Sam Pig was quite frightened, but the water-maid only laughed gently.

'Good-bye, Sam. Good-bye, Brock. I shall never forget you. I shall look for you by the river. Good-bye.'

She took up her harp and played as she swam through the water, and the river heard, and hushed, listening to her voice.

> 'Deep flowing river,
>   Oh wide green water,
>   I am come hither,
>   I am your daughter.
>   Farewell springs and streams,
>   Water, dear water,
>   I see you in dreams,
>   I am your daughter.'

She glided softly back to the river and the waves flowed over her. For a moment the gold harp was held aloft, and then it too disappeared. The river gave a triumphant chuckle of satisfaction. The storm died down, and Sam and Brock turned to go home.

'Here's one of the flowers she dropped,' said Sam, picking up a yellow flag. 'I shall keep this, Brock.'

Brock nodded. 'Lovely creatures, are water-maids, Sam, but they are not for the likes of us.'

'I 'spose not,' sighed Sam. 'But I'm glad we saw her again, Brock.'

Dinner for Brock

Into the wood went a small stout figure, walking carefully, glancing down at the burden he carried. It was our little Sam Pig, taking Brock's dinner to the Badger, who was working among the trees. The dinner was in a white basin, with a saucer on the top, and it was tied up in a red handkerchief. Anyone could see it was something special by the way Sam carried it, neither swinging nor swaying it. The corners of the handkerchief were tied together to form a handle. Sam felt very important as he walked along the track. He had seen plumbers and masons and farm labourers carrying their dinners in that way.

Inside the basin was a hot-pot, that Ann had made for Brock that morning. Although Tom Pig was the cook in the little household, Ann sometimes came forward to try her hand at a tasty dish for old Brock the Badger. Yes, that very same morning Ann had made it and Sam Pig had helped her. Ann sang a little ditty as she cooked, and this is what she sang:

> 'Half a pound of twopenny rice,
> Half a pound of treacle,

> Half a pound of what-you-like,
> Pop goes the weasel.'

Ann had boiled the twopenny rice, and mixed it with the treacle, and added half a pound of what-you-like to the dish. It made the delicious hot-pot, that sent curls of fragrant steam through the handkerchief, flowing up among the trees like incense.

Sam sniffed and sniffed, and the rabbits came out and sniffed, and even the weasels poked their cruel, slender heads out of holes and twitched their wicked nostrils.

There was a rustle in the undergrowth, and every animal faded away into the earth, except Sam, who marched on, trying to be very brave as he glanced sideways. Perhaps it was a wolf or a bear coming lolloping after Brock's hot-pot. Sam was ready to defend the pot with his life if necessary.

It was only the Fox, prowling about, attracted by the good, rich smell. The Fox looked slyly at Sam and stepped lightly up to him, tiptoeing in the bracken like a dancer, not walking in good English manner like little Sam.

'Hello, Sam Pig. What's that you're carrying so carefully? A brace of pheasants in the pot?' he asked.

'Hot-pot for Brock the Badger,' said Sam proudly.

'Give me a taste, Sam,' wheedled the Fox. 'I've not had a square meal for a week.'

'Can't!' answered Sam. 'It's not mine to give. Brock is waiting for it.'

'Hum!' thought the Fox. 'If Brock is near I must be quiet. No chance of taking it.'

Then he said aloud, 'What's it made of? I never smelled such a grand smell as comes from that little pot you're carrying there.'

'I'll sing you the song of it,' said Sam proudly. and he put down the pot and sang:

> 'Half a pound of twopenny rice,
> Half a pound of treacle,
> Half a pound of what-you-like,
> Pop goes the weasel.'

'Indeed! And what kind of a thing is what-you-like?' asked the Fox.

'It's mushrooms,' answered Sam, picking up the basin. 'Brock likes mushrooms, so we put them in for him.'

'If I made it I should put half a pound of roast duck into it, Sam, or half a pound of rabbit,' said the Fox. 'You and Ann know nothing about cookery. Let me help you to make a hot-pot, a real good one, for Brock.'

'For Brock?' asked Sam, hesitating.

'Yes, for Brock. I have a recipe which belonged to my grandmother. I should like to teach it to you.'

'Oh, thank you,' said Sam. 'Come along when we

'Hello, Sam Pig. What's that you're carrying so carefully?'

can have the kitchen to ourselves. I never get the
chance to do any real cooking.'

So the Fox galloped away and Sam went on
through the wood to the clearing where Brock was
working. There was Brock cutting down small trees,
making a rough wooden summerhouse. The Badger
put down his axe and welcomed Sam.

'Good lad, Sam. I was just ready for my dinner.
I could smell it coming. The wind caught it and
brought it to me. What is it?'

'A hot-pot, Brock. Ann made it.'

Brock untied the handkerchief and sat down on a
stump with the basin between his knees. He poured
out some of the stew into the saucer, and offered it to
Sam.

'You have a taste, Sam. There's more than I want.'

They lapped it up and licked out the basin and
saucer in the way of all well-brought-up animals. In
a circle round them sat the small creatures of the
woodland, watching and waiting, but there was
nothing left for them.

'Very tasty, very sweet,' said Brock.

'Very sweet, very tasty,' said Sam.

'Now, Sam, you shall help me,' said Brock.
'Trim the logs while I build the walls. Here's a bill-
hook. Do it like this.'

The Badger showed Sam how to swish off the little
branches and make the logs clean. Then he went on
with the walls. Quite soon the little summerhouse was

ready for its roof. Brock fastened branches across it, and there it was, a house in the forest ready for anyone who wanted to spend a night in comfort. There was a door with a wooden bolt and hinges of bark, and a knocker made out of a piece of oak. Brock had carved it in the shape of a fox's head, and Sam laughed when he saw how the jaw moved on a string.

'I met the Fox today,' said he to Brock. 'He said he would help me to make a hot-pot, a very good recipe, handed down to him by his grandmother.'

'His grandmother!' muttered Brock.

A few days later Sam met the Fox in the wood.

'Sam Pig, I'm ready to show you how to cook. I've got my grandmother's recipe in my pocket,' said the Fox, lightly skipping on one toe and swishing his brush like a fan.

'Come home with me now, Mister Fox,' invited Sam. 'There's nobody in the house. They've all gone to see Brock's summerhouse in the wood. Ann has made a carpet of rushes for the floor and Bill and Tom are taking the besoms to clean the leaves away.'

'I accept your invitation with great pleasure,' simpered the Fox. Back to the cottage they ran, the Fox leading the way, for he wanted to get the cooking done before the family returned to turn him out.

'Where are the scales?' he asked, as soon as they entered the kitchen. 'You must weigh everything carefully. It is most important.'

'We usually guesses,' said Sam, 'but we have

some scales somewhere for things like half a pound of this and that.'

He got the little wooden see-saw which balanced on a wedge of wood, and he showed it to the Fox.

'You put a half-pound stone on one end, and the thing to be weighed on the other. Then you try and try till the two balance,' he explained.

'Very clever,' said the Fox. 'Show me the half-pound weight.'

Sam looked everywhere, but he couldn't find it, and the reason was that the Fox had seen it first and hidden it.

'Never mind, Sam. We can manage. I am full of ideas,' the Fox reassured the little Pig. 'I can do a half-pound press.'

He glanced at the sack of rice on the bench and the great tin of treacle which Brock had bought at the market.

'Half a pound of twopenny rice,' said the Fox. 'That's how my grandmother's recipe begins too. You put the rice on the see-saw – I mean the scales, and I'll hold the other end.'

So Sam put a few fistfuls of rice on the long see-saw, and the Fox pressed down his end.

'More rice, Sam. It isn't half a pound yet. It doesn't make my end go down,' said the Fox.

Sam brought more and more, but the Fox pressed harder, and it wasn't till the sack was nearly emptied that at last the wooden scales balanced.

'It looks a big half-pound,' remarked Sam.

'Yes. It's the weather,' said the Fox. 'Sometimes it makes half-pounds shrink to nothing and sometimes they grow. It all depends. Your scales are right, aren't they?'

'Oh yes,' said Sam. 'Tom and Ann use them.'

'Next get the treacle,' said the Fox, licking his lips. 'I think you might put the tin on the see-saw, and we shall see how much to take out.'

Sam carried the heavy tin and placed it carefully on the scales. The Fox pressed his end as before, and the two sides balanced.

'Exactly half a pound. Good guess,' said he.

'But – but – but—' began Sam.

'Exactly,' said the Fox. 'Now for the half-pound of what-you-like. That is the special part of my grandmother's recipe. Shut your eyes, Sam, while I look round for what-I-like.'

Obediently Sam shut his eyes and the Fox peered round. There were no ducks hanging in the larder, but there was a basket of new-laid eggs, and some golden butter which had just come from the farm. The Fox brought them out and put them on the table.

'This is what-I-like,' said he, calling to Sam.

'But those eggs have to last all week,' stammered Sam.

'My grandmother's recipe distinctly says eggs and butter for what-you-like,' replied the Fox coldly. 'We will now mix all together for the hot-pot, Sam.

I think your bath would hold them comfortably.'

He weighed the butter and eggs on the scales, and of course they weighed half a pound when he pressed the end of the wood. Then he poured the rice, the treacle, the eggs and butter into Sam's bath and beat them with a wooden spoon. He heated them over the fire for a few minutes, and Sam stood watching with admiration. It was a hot-pot big enough for everybody to have a good helping, and then a second helping afterwards.

'Now for a pudding-cloth,' said the Fox.

'We haven't got one,' said Sam. 'No, not a pudding-cloth. We've got a dish-cloth to wash up, but no pudding-cloth.'

'Anything will do to boil the pudding in,' said the Fox, gaily. 'A sheet from your bed, a blanket, a quilt. It is going to be a fine hot-pot of a pudding. Go and fetch the cloth, Sam.'

Sam went reluctantly upstairs. He felt uncomfortable as he dragged a sheet from his bed. Ann was very fussy about sheets. Usually Sam slept on straw, but lately he had had a sheet. He didn't know what Ann would say when she found a pudding hot-pot wrapped up in it, as sticky as could be. Sam pulled the sheet after him and caught his foot in the folds. Downstairs he clattered, bumping and banging on every step.

When he disentangled himself the Fox had disappeared, with the bath and the pudding. Sam ran

to the door. Away in the distance he saw the red
figure of the sly fellow dragging the bath into the
wood.

'Oh dear me!' sighed Sam. 'What will they say!
Half a pound of twopenny rice gone, half a pound
of treacle gone, half a pound of eggs and butter gone,
and my bath too.'

He tidied away the mess and put the sheet back on

the bed. Then he sat down, a miserable pigling, to wait for the return of the family.

Half an hour later they came in. Ann Pig came first with an armful of rushes to make another rug for the kitchen floor. Tom Pig came next with a bundle of firewood. Bill Pig carried a honeycomb from the wild bees' nest. Last of all came Brock, dragging Sam's bath with the great pudding hot-pot in it.

'Oh! Oh!' cried Sam. 'Where did you find that, Brock?'

'We heard a noise in the wood,' said Brock, 'and we went to see what it was. Such a squealing and squeaking as never was! There stood the Fox, with the bath, and a host of weasels leaping round, crying for their dinner. They said it was theirs, and he said it was his, because he had made it, so I went up and said it was mine.'

'And Brock won,' said Tom, simply.

'Yes, I won,' said Brock.

That night they all ate the delicious pudding hot-pot, and they voted thanks to the Fox's grandmother for her nice recipe, although it had taken their week's store.

When they had finished they all sang the old song:

> 'Half a pound of twopenny rice,
> Half a pound of treacle,
> Half a pound of what-you-like.
> Pop goes the weasel.'

'Why was the half-pound such a big one when the Fox weighed the rice?' asked Sam.

I leave you to guess Brock's answer.

The Christmas Box

Sam Pig was walking home from the farm one winter's day with a bottle of ginger wine under his arm. It was a present from Mrs Greensleeves, for the family. There was a rustle, and the Red Fox stood in the path waiting for Sam.

'I want to have a word with you, Sam Pig,' said the Fox.

'Yes?' said Sam, hopefully.

'You once sang a very nice song to me. It was a Christmas song, a kind of carol. It was a song full of promises. Do you remember it, Sam?'

Sam shook his head. He sang so many little tunes, he forgot them as soon as he made them up.

'Try to remember, Sam,' urged the Fox, blocking the way so that Sam couldn't get past. 'Try to recollect your song. If you don't remember I must nudge your memory.'

Sam didn't like the Fox's tone, so he made a great effort, and sang this song in a faltering voice:

> 'Dear Mister Fox,
> He opens iron locks.
> He eats all the geese,
> The hens and turkey-cocks.'

'Is that the song?' he asked timidly.

'No!' said the Fox sharply, and he gave Sam a nip. 'No! That is an insulting song. I love geese and hens and turkey-cocks. I don't get the chance to eat them. No! This is what you sang to me that day, long ago, when you were in the woods looking for besom trees. This is the song, Sam Pig.'

The Fox sang the little song in a sharp harsh voice, and Sam sighed as he listened.

> 'Dear Mister Fox,
> He needs a Christmas Box,
> A coat and a hat,
> And a pair of yellow socks.'

Yes, Sam remembered he had sung this silly song when he was in a tight corner, with the Fox pulling his ear and mocking him.

'Christmas is coming, Sam Pig. I want a coat, a hat and a pair of yellow socks. Warmth and comfort there, Sam. See you get them for me,' said the Fox.

Sam stared without speaking. He felt more and more uncomfortable.

'I shall expect my Christmas Box, Sam,' leered the Fox. He took Sam's ginger wine from under the little Pig's arm, and drained the bottle. He choked a little and coughed, and threw the empty bottle away.

'Too much warmth there. I shall enjoy my present, Sam.' He disappeared into the thick bushes, and Sam walked sadly on.

'Confusticate that Fox!' he groaned. 'He's an interfering busy-body, spoiling my outing, and re-membering things I had forgotten. I am the most miserable of piglings. Where can I get a coat and hat and a pair of yellow socks? Socks don't grow on bushes, or hats on trees.'

'Oh yes, they do!' said a wee small voice, and Sam Pig started in surprise. He looked at the tree tops and down to the ground but he could see nobody.

'Oh yes, they do! They do, Sam Pig!' squeaked a tiny voice, and Sam scratched his head and looked behind and before.

'That's very odd. I thought I heard somebody speak,' said he.

'They do! They do! They do!' sang the voice, and Sam stared at the stump of a tree from which the voice came.

'Do what?' he asked, confused.

'Socks grow on gorse bushes and coats on holly trees,' answered the shrill piping cry.

Out of a hole in the rough stump came Jemima Mouse, the little friend who once lived in Sam's trouser pocket. Her whiskers were sharp, her eyes bright and her hands clean.

'Oh Jemima!' cried Sam joyfully. 'I am glad to see you. What are you doing here? You were living in an old boot down the lane the last time I saw you.'

The mouse sat up and curled her tail about her like a shawl. She nodded her tiny head at Sam.

'I flitted from there. I had so many children there wasn't room in that boot, so now we all live in this tree,' said Jemima. 'I heard you talking to the Fox, Sam Pig. The Fox is no friend of mine. Take my advice. Listen to my words.'

Sam sat down on the trunk and the mouse whispered into his ear. It was necessary to speak softly lest the Fox should hear. He might be round the corner, listening, so the mouse whispered the advice.

'I understand, Jemima,' said Sam.

He ran all the way home to tell Sister Ann about the plan. They talked it over together.

'I can make them if you get the materials,' said Ann, and she fetched her wicker workbasket and sharpened her needles on the stone and counted her bobbins of horse-hair thread.

'Sharp as thorns,' said she, as she touched the needle points.

Sam Pig went out with his axe and cut branches of green holly from the trees in the wood. He dragged them home to Ann. She stripped the pointed leaves from the branches and sewed them together with her strong thread. She made from them a long green coat, prickly and stiff like a coat of mail, shining like

metal where the light caught the glossy surface of the hard leaves.

Then she wove an ivy-leaf hat, smooth and strong-smelling, with a cluster of black ivy-berries in the brim.

Sam went to the lanes where the bushes of gorse still had some yellow flowers, although it was winter.

'When the gorse is out of flower, then kissing's out of season,' says the old proverb, and everyone knows kissing is never out of season. So Sam picked the long spiny trails of gorse with the golden pea-flowers scenting them.

Ann frowned as she pricked her hands with them.

'How can I knit a pair of socks from these, Sam?' she asked.

Sam thought for a minute and twisted the flowery sprays together. They stuck as if they had been sewn, for the thorns locked into one another and couldn't be separated.

'I can do it, Ann,' cried he. 'I can make the socks without any knitting needles. Just watch me.'

He pressed the thorns and flowers into the shape of up-standing yellow socks.

'Good enough for any Fox to walk about in, if he can wear them,' said Bill Pig, examining them.

'It's like wearing a pincushion,' cried Tom, pushing a foot in the sock and hopping out again.

'That's what I want them to be,' laughed Sam. 'The Fox must wear something uncomfortable for once.'

The next day Sam carried the holly coat, the ivy hat and the gorse-flower socks to the wood. The coat was bright green, glittering in the sun like chain mail. The socks were covered with little scented flowers smelling of honey. The hat was a marvel of ivy leaves. It was a fine-looking present for Mister Fox.

There was nobody to be seen, so Sam laid them near the tree stump where little Jemima lived. With them he left a letter.

'Dear Mister Fox,
Here's your Christmas box.
A holly coat, an ivy hat,
And a pair of gorsey socks.'

From the hollow in the tree came the faint snores of Jemima and her fourteen children. Sam dropped a tiny loaf down the hole and went away.

Presently the sharp nose of the Fox came peering round.

'Ha! What's this! A green coat and hat? A pair of yellow socks? They are from little Sam Pig.'

He read the letter and smiled. 'A holly coat won't wear out. An ivy hat is fashionable and gorsey socks – well, they are always in season.'

He slipped the coat on his back and popped the hat on his head.

'Ugh! There's something sharp in the coat lining,' he muttered. 'Ann Pig must have left her needle sticking there. She has left her pins, her scissors, her bodkin, and stiletto, all pricking me.'

He wriggled uncomfortably as the holly spines pierced his thick fur. The yellow socks stood upright like gold boots and he put them on. First one foot went inside and then the other. His nose wrinkled as a gorse spine stuck into him.

'Ann Pig's left her knitting needles in the socks. She's left a thousand pins,' cried the Fox, leaping up and dancing with pain. The more he danced, the fiercer clung the yellow socks. He tried to pull them

'Lemme go! Lemme go! Ah! Oh-oh-oh!' he squealed.

off, but they were tightly fastened to his fur, tangled in the hairs, with every yellow flower and green spike piercing his legs.

'Lemme go! Lemme go! Ah! Oh-oh-oh!' he squealed, and he flung the hat away and dragged the coat from his back.

'Oh, Sam Pig! If I could catch you now, I'd make you pay for this,' shouted the Fox.

Sam Pig rolled on the ground with laughter, and stuffed his handkerchief in his mouth to keep in his cries of joy. Even the mouse stopped snoring and came to see what was happening.

The Fox was dancing in the yellow socks, shrieking revenge on Sam Pig.

'If I get hold of you, Sam Pig, I'll give you a Christmas box that you'll remember all your days,' threatened the Fox.

But Sam sang another song.

> 'Poor Mister Fox,
>   He's got his Christmas Box.
>   A holly coat, an ivy hat,
>   A pair of gorsey socks,'

sang Sam, leaping up and running away.

The Fox moaned and sat down on the tree trunk. Slowly he pulled the socks off his feet, prickle by prickle, flower by yellow flower. The holly coat lay in a heap, the ivy hat beside it.

'Sam Pig's a regular varmint. A regular varmint,'

he mumbled to himself. 'I'll never trust him again.'

He limped home and bathed his sore feet in the stream. He asked his wife to make a poultice for his toes. He called his children to pull out the prickly holly leaves which were entangled in his back and sides.

'Never put your trust in a fat little pig, children,' said he, shaking a warning finger at them, and the young foxes promised.

'Not even if he promises you a Christmas box,' said the Fox.

'No. Not even if he promises us a Christmas box,' repeated the young foxes, but all the same they wished Sam Pig would give them a nice present on Christmas morning.

The Train Journey

Across the valleys and over the woods, away on the horizon there was a hill blue as a cornflower. Sam asked his sister about it, but she knew nothing.

'It's over the hill and far away,' said she.

'Why is it blue?' asked Sam.

'Perhaps it is covered with bluebells,' said Ann.

'No. It is the distance that lends the enchanting colour,' said Brock.

Sam determined to visit this distant hill. He went off one day, and walked and walked and climbed till he got there. It wasn't blue at all. It was green with trees and grass and bracken. Sam climbed to the top, where there was a look-out tree, with names carved on its trunk. He gazed over the valleys and moors. Surely he could see all the world from that hill top! As he stood there, a solitary little figure with his trousers flapping in the wind, seeking the familiar spots he knew, the cottages and farms and villages among the hills, he heard a faint sound. He saw a great beast with a long body and flaming head come out of a hole in a hill and run swiftly and smoothly along to another hole, when it disappeared. It gave a shrill cry as it dived into the ground, and then all was silence except for the singing of birds.

Sam gasped!

'A dragon who lives in a hill,' thought he. 'A fiery dragon! It may be the brother of my own dragon that went back to sleep in the wood for a thousand years.'

Sam ran down the hill and walked the long way home, anxious to tell his family all about it. It was indeed a great adventure to have seen a dragon, and heard its cry.

'Don't you go and bring that dragon here,' said Bill crossly, when Sam told his tale. The family wasn't pleased to hear about the dragon.

'We want no more dragons. Farmer Greensleeves was quite upset when your dragon ate his cow, Primrose,' said Tom Pig.

'The dragon was hungry,' said Sam. 'You can't expect them to go without anything to eat for a thousand years and not be hungry.'

'Well, keep your dragon,' said Bill. 'We don't want another, thank you.'

When Brock came home that night they told him about the fiery dragon, with smoke coming from its nostrils, and a shriek from its throat, roaring across the valley from one hole to another.

'That wasn't a dragon,' said Brock, thoughtfully puffing his pipe. 'No. That was a train with an

engine and all, going to carry people from one place to another.'

The little pigs were amazed. They wanted to know more but Brock shook his head. He didn't like the monsters. They stayed on their own iron road, but if anyone got in their way there was no escape. He knew a good old Badger who was killed by walking on their track. Best keep away from such dangers.

Sam Pig listened to all this. There were many things he wanted to know but Brock wouldn't say any more.

'Time for all good pigs to go to bed,' said he, firmly. 'Time for sleep if you want to be fresh in the morning. No more talk about trains or dragons either.'

Sam thought all the more about them, and the next time he met Sally the Mare he questioned her.

'I've often seen a train,' said Sally calmly. 'My master rides in one every week to the big market in the town. I take him to the station and he gets in the train. At night I meet him and bring him home again. Jack drives me, and there is always great fun and excitement at the farm when we return. Master's pockets are full, his basket is full. He talks for hours of what he has seen and done.'

'When do you go again?' asked Sam.

'Tomorrow,' said Sally. 'It's the day for market tickets. Cheap fares on market day.'

'Oh!' whispered Sam, slowly. 'Oh!'

He walked home by the woods and sat under the trees thinking about it. He made his plans. Everything must be secret, for he was certain that Brock would stop him. He made up his young determined mind that he would ride in a train, to see what it was like inside that flaming monster.

The next morning he got up at dawn, dressed himself carefully in his Sunday clothes, put a clean handkerchief in his pocket and a big hat on his head, and looked in the money-box. There was one penny, with a hole in it, so he threaded it on a string and wore it round his neck. He filled a basket with ferns and fox-gloves and cabbages, and he was ready. He trotted quickly over the fields to the farm, with the basket on his arm. He hid in the drive and waited.

Soon Sally came down the road with the farmer and Jack in the spring cart. Farmer Greensleeves was dressed in his best coat, and he wore a stiff black hat and a white collar and tie. Sam longed for a white collar, and he whipped his handkerchief out of his pocket and wrapped it round his neck.

As soon as the farmer drove by, Sam came out and clung to the back of the cart. That was easy enough, there was a handle and an iron step. Sam swung him-self up and sat there, dangling his legs in great content, with the basket on his knee.

Away they drove, down the hills and along the valleys, in and out of villages, Sally trotting at a regular steady pace, the farmer and Jack talking of this and of that, little Sam clinging to the back of the vehicle, hidden by the cart-tail.

At last they arrived at the station, and Sally stopped in the busy yard among cabs and carriages and carts. Sam slipped away and watched the farmer alight. When Sally was alone and the cart had been emptied of its baskets and passengers, Sam stepped up to the mare for a last word with her.

'Goodness gracious, Sam Pig! What are you doing here? cried the mare in astonishment.

'I'm going in the train, Sally.'

'Never! Never! Sam Pig! You are a caution, Sam Pig!'

'Good-bye, Sally.'

'Good-bye and good luck, Sam. I hope we shall meet again,' murmured Sally, still bewildered.

Sam ran after the farmer and heard him ask for a market ticket to Lower Cheeping. He saw the silver coin put down in the little wired window, and he sighed, for he hadn't a shilling in the world, and this coin was something else, very big and grand.

He followed Farmer Greensleeves to the platform and stood near, but not too close. He was happy and excited to see the little crowd of farmers, drovers, and country folk going to the market town with baskets, just like Sam's basket. He was glad he had brought a basket of green stuff to shield himself against staring eyes.

There was a clatter as a signal fell; the porter came pushing a barrow of luggage, the station-master walked about in his fine uniform. Sam shrank shyly back and sat down on a seat next to an old woman. He felt safer there, away from the legs and sticks of all the crowd.

There was a rush and a roar and the great engine came into the station. Sam trembled and shook, for he thought the iron beast was going to run over the platform and devour everybody. Instead, it drew up like a patient old cart horse and waited, puffing and panting and blowing steam from its head. Sam

Sam trembled and shook, for he thought the iron beast was going to run over the platform.

wanted to go and look at it, but everyone was busy climbing into the carriages. The little pig couldn't find Farmer Greensleeves, so he ran after the old woman whose wide skirts were mounting the steps. Close to her went Sam, clinging to her, and hauling his basket after him. He scrambled into the carriage and sat down close to her side. She was so large he was half hidden by her dress. It was just as well, as it gave him a chance to look about him.

'Good morning, Mrs Wildgoose,' said the lady opposite, and Sam's old lady said 'Good day to you, Mrs Dobbie. It's a fine day but we want a drop of rain.'

'Yes, we could do with a nice drop of rain,' said Mrs Dobbie.

'It will rain on Saturday when the moon changes,' said Sam boldly. 'Brock says so.'

'That's true, sonny. Change of moon will do it,' agreed Mrs Dobbie.

'How are your pigs, Mrs Wildgoose?' she went on.

'Middlin'. They's fattening only middlin'. What with the state of market and the price of meal, it's a bad lookout for pigs.'

'So 'tis,' agreed the other.

'A bad lookout for pigs,' murmured Sam, and he made himself very small and looked out of the window nervously.

'That young fellow your grandson?' asked Mrs Dobbie.

'No,' said Mrs Wildgoose, glancing down at Sam.
'He's nothing to do with me. He's on his own.'

She lowered her voice. 'Very homely face. Very
plain!'

'And what might your name be?' she asked Sam.

'Sam, please ma'am,' replied Sam.

'Sam what?'

'Just plain Sam,' murmured Sam, and they all
laughed. It seemed to put them in a good humour,
for one of the people brought out a bag of humbugs
and gave it to Sam.

'And what are you going to buy at the market,
Sam?' asked Mrs Wildgoose kindly.

'A pennorth of goodies,' whispered Sam.

He turned his head to the window and gazed out
in surprise at the scenery which had taken to itself
wings. It was flying past; trees and houses, bushes
and barns, all trundled along with invisible wings on
their shoulders. Far away he could see the hill with
the look-out tree from which he had first caught a
glimpse of a train. In a minute they dived with a
terrible roar into darkness, but a lamp in the roof
lighted the carriage. Sam stared at the little star
above his head. Under the earth they were, among
gnomes and dwarfs, and nobody saw them except
Sam. He peered into the tunnel and thought bright
eyes were watching him and small dark humped
figures were leaping beside the train. Then out they
rushed to the light, and there was a new scene to

watch. So on they went, stopping at country stations, making room for more passengers, squeezing up and laughing together. What a pleasant lot of folk they were, these humans, thought Sam!

Everybody was going to the market, and they gave each other advice and spoke of prices and food and inns.

'I has my bit of dinner at the Bull,' said one. 'It's good and cheap.'

'Oh, I goes to the Red Lion,' said another.

'And I goes to the Blue Boar,' said a third.

Sam Pig listened, and Mrs Wildgoose suddenly leaned to him.

'Where are you going to have your bite, my dear?'

She said the words so kindly with such a warm burring sound on the 'dear' that Sam answered readily. 'I might go to the Green Dragon,' said he, hoping there was such a place.

'Very expensive,' murmured Mrs Wildgoose. 'You go to the Boar.'

The scene was changing, there were more houses than Sam had ever seen, spinning past the windows.

'Tickets please,' said a collector, coming along the platform of the next station. 'Get your tickets ready.'

'Get your ticket out, sonny,' said Mrs Wildgoose to Sam.

'Please ma'am, I haven't got one,' said Sam, looking up at her with blue eyes innocent and wide.

'Not got one? Why, you can't travel without 'un.'

she cried and all the people in the carriage looked at Sam.

'You ought to have got a ticket, sonny. Why didn't you get one? Didn't you have time?'

'I only had a penny,' said Sam, showing his dear old penny with a hole in it hanging round his neck by a string.

'Tickets, please. Tickets, please.' Doors were banging and steps were coming nearer.

'Here, hide under the seat,' whispered kind Mrs Wildgoose, spreading out her skirts, and Sam crawled underneath and lay there sniffing the dust and boot blacking and the smell of thick heavy skirts.

'Come out, all safe,' called the people when the ticket collector had gone and the train had started once more. They reached their parcels from the racks, and stood up, for they were getting near Lower Cheeping.

'Lower Cheeping. All change. Lower Cheeping,' cried porters, and everybody tumbled out in a great hurry. Sam loitered behind and went to see the engine. He watched the fireman rub the brass, and wipe his oily hands. He gave the engine a pat on its side. Then, happy and gay, he went off to the great market.

The size of it took Sam's breath away. A square was filled with stalls, and people, and pens of sheep and pens of cows. Sam walked about, peering and prying, sometimes putting out his tongue for a lick at a carrot or turnip, sometimes staring with longing at the heaps of sugar sticks and candy.

A woman stopped him and turned over his ferns and foxgloves.

'How much for your roots?' she asked.

'What you like,' said Sam.

'I'll take the lot for a shilling,' said she, and Sam nodded vigorously. A shilling! It was a fortune for Sam. He emptied the basket, and pocketed the coin, with many thanks.

On he went, with the empty basket slung over his arm, and now he felt a rich little pig, who could buy everything he desired. He was getting hungry, so he joined the country folk who thronged round a coffee stall. How delicious was the hot coffee with plenty of sugar, and the big currant bun which he bought! He was eating and drinking, when he felt a hand on his arm, and he looked up in a sudden fright.

'Ah! It is! It is my little Pigwiggin! It is indeed,' said a quiet voice at his side. There stood the Old Woman who lived in the wood, little Sam's friend of long ago.

'Oh, ma'am. I am glad to see you,' cried Sam. 'I didn't know you in your bonnet.'

'Nor did I know my Pigwiggin, but I had a suspicion when I saw little trotters and check trousers, and big ears. I thought it must be my Pigwiggin, come to market.'

'I've sold my basket of ferns and foxgloves and cabbages,' said Sam happily, showing his coins to the old woman.

'We are both rich, Sam. We'll have a fine time together. We'll go on the dobby horses, and eat ice cream and see all there is to be seen, for I want a young merry Pigwiggin to keep me company.'

So Sam and the old country woman went through the market together, buying pear drops and brandy snaps and mint rock. They rode on the roundabouts, each perched on a fine dobby horse with red nostrils and grey mane. They attracted some attention, for the Old Woman wore an antiquated cloak and a bonnet of a hundred years ago, and Sam – well – he was just Sam Pig, with his little pink snout and bright eyes and flapping ears half concealed under the big hat. People were staring at them as the wooden horses spun round and round, asking if they were part of the show, whether they had escaped from a menagerie. The Old Woman thought it was time to move away.

They wandered off to the town to look at the shops. Ah! Sam had never seen such things before, and he was excited over gas-pipes in a plumber's and over feathered hats in a French milliner's.

'Would you like to buy presents for your family, Sam?' asked the Old Woman. 'I have brought my teapot full of money with me. I never spend anything in the forest. Choose what you like.'

Wasn't that nice for Sam Pig? He didn't know what to buy and the Old Woman had to help him.

'A blue straw bonnet with red roses for Sister Ann,' said Sam, pointing to a little bonnet in a shop window.

So inside the shop they went, and the Old Woman took the teapot from under her cloak and paid for the blue straw bonnet.

'Anything else, madam?' asked the young lady assistant, as she dropped the bonnet in a wide paper bag. Her eyes never left the cauliflower-teapot which was filled with sovereigns.

'We will get seven pocket handkerchiefs for Bill,' said the Old Woman. 'One for each day of the week.'

Sam chose seven colours – red, blue, green, yellow, violet, brown and orange – for Brother Bill.

'What would Tom like?' asked the Old Woman.

'A new frying-pan I think,' said Sam. 'Ours has a hole, and things fall through it when Tom is cooking.'

So they chose a nice iron frying-pan, the largest size there was.

Brock's present was the most difficult, for Sam kept changing his mind. He wavered between a briar pipe, a top hat, a walking stick and a tin trumpet.

'I know of something for Brock,' said the Old Woman. She took Sam down a street of crooked houses, bending over to talk to each other, with carved timbers and overhanging gables.

'This is the Street of Old Days,' she told Sam. They went along the cobbles, to an old curiosity shop. The window was filled with strange things, jewels piled on a dish, toys and dolls that had belonged to queens. The Old Woman lifted the latch and went down two stairs to a dusky room, and Sam stumbled after her.

A man in a black skull-cap came forward, and the Old Woman spoke a word or two in a language Sam didn't understand. The man nodded and looked at Sam, and nodded again.

'Something for a Badger?' he asked. 'Yes. I have just the thing. An old curiosity, with a bit of magic in it.'

He went into a corner and brought a box. Inside was a glass ball, which he lifted out with care. The little globe held a tiny ship sailing on the sea. When he shook the ball the ship seemed to come alive. The waves rolled, the ship moved onward, and sailors ran up the rigging. Little fish appeared in the water, and dolphins sported round the sides of the vessel. For a few minutes the life went on, and then all was quiet again. It was a miracle of a ball, and Sam knew that Brock would be delighted.

'And now a present for you, little Sam,' said the Old Woman.

The man brought a frog mug for Sam to see. It was a china mug with a green china frog at the bottom to startle the drinker.

'You will always have a laugh in your mug when you drink from the spring,' said the Old Woman.

The old curiosity man showed Sam and his friend many of the treasures of his shop. There was a nightingale which popped out of a musical box and sang, and a wooden bear in a cage, and a mug which played a tune when you put it down.

He took no money for the ball and mug, only a pinch of herbs the Old Woman brought from her pocket. They brought sleep to the weary, he said, and health and fortune, which was better than gold.

They said good-bye and went away, back to the market-place, with their fairings packed in Sam's basket. 'It's dinner-time, Sam. Where shall we go?' asked the Old Woman.

'To the Green Dragon,' said Sam promptly, but when they arrived outside the hotel they were both too frightened to enter.

'To the Blue Boar,' said Sam, and there next door was the homely little inn with a Pig in a blue coat on the sign board. In the cosy room sat Mrs Wildgoose and Mrs Dobbie, and Farmer Greensleeves as well.

'How did you get here, Sam?' asked the Farmer. 'You'll get lost in this great place.'

'I'm taking care of him, Farmer Greensleeves,' said the Old Woman, patting Sam's arm.

They sat down to a little table with a white cloth, a salt cellar and pepper pot. All these were strange to

Sam. He tasted the salt and sniffed at the pepper and decided he wouldn't have them. A plate of porridge followed by ice cream was more to his fancy.

Everybody looked at Sam, and a fine lady sniffed and drew her skirts away, but little Sam beamed round at the company, unconscious of his odd appearance.

Out came the teapot again, as the Old Woman paid for their dinners, and Sam insisted on putting his change into the china cauliflower-teapot.

They went to the river and watched the rowing boats and the little paddle steamer. They walked up the narrow steps to the watch towers of the walled town, and the Old Woman told Sam stories of days when robber bands laid siege to those walls.

It was time to go home, and they walked back to the station.

'Sam. Would you like to ride on the engine?' asked the Old Woman. 'The engine-driver is my sister Matilda's grandson, and he will let you ride on the footplate if I ask him.'

'Oh, ma'am, I should like that,' cried Sam. 'I should indeed.'

The Old Woman went down the platform and had a word with the bright-eyed young man in the engine.

'I'll take him, so long as nobody sees. Passengers not allowed on engines.'

'Sam Pig is no passenger. He's just a Pigwiggin.

There's no law against Pigwiggins in engines, is there?'

'No,' pondered the man. 'There isn't. I'll take him, Great-aunt Tabitha.'

'Good lad. Here's a something for you,' said the Old Woman. She passed a gold coin from the teapot to the engine-driver's hand.

Sam climbed up and sat among the coal. The train started with roars and pants as real as those of a live dragon.

'I'm going. I think I am. I think I am. I think I am,' Sam heard it say. The engine-driver soon forgot about Sam, he was busy attending to his work and Sam never spoke. He was intent on the engine. He could understand its language. The engine was pleased to see Sam Pig. It began to talk to him, chuffing away, telling of all its difficulties, its loads, its adventures. It spoke of the curious things that had happened in its life, and all it had seen as it sped through fields and woods, alongside rivers and by canals.

Sam Pig told the engine of his own life far away in the woods with Brock the Badger and the family.

The engine had never had such a time, for nobody ever talked to it except the engine-driver, who called it George and grumbled at it.

All the way they chatted, and Sam would have been left in the train if it hadn't been for the Old Woman who came to find him. He leapt down just in

He leapt down just in time, and the engine-driver tossed his basket after him.

time, and the engine-driver tossed his basket after him.

'Blest if I didn't forget all about you,' said the man. 'Been to sleep, I suppose. The noise makes folk sleepy.'

Sam nodded good-bye to the engine and hurried out of the station to the farm cart. The Old Woman was already climbing to the seat beside the farmer and Jack. Sam squatted on the back step, and Sally turned her head to look at him.

'Well, Sam Pig. I thought I had seen the last of you,' said she. 'You've turned up like a bad penny.'

'So you came to the station with me this morning, unbeknownst, did you, Sam?' called the farmer.

'Yes, master, thank you,' cried Sam.

'Let me know the next time, and you can ride by my side,' said the farmer.

'Thank you, master,' said Sam.

They drove along the winding roads home. At the cross-roads the Old Woman got down and said good-bye.

'Don't go a-roaming by yourself, little Pigwiggin, or you may rue it,' she called to Sam. 'Just let us know.'

'All right, thank you,' said Sam, waving his dirty hand.

When they reached the drive, Sam got down. He thanked the farmer and went off home with his basket of fairings on his arm. His legs were tired, his head in a whirl with all he had seen, his face was smudged with coal dust, his hands black as a nigger's.

What a welcome there was for the small traveller when he arrived!

'I rode on the engine and talked to it,' said Sam, as he drank his tea. 'It was quite tame, and it ate coal and drank water. It doesn't eat cows, because I asked it. It sleeps in a shed, and it has a man to dress it and wash it and feed it.'

'What was its name?' asked Tom Pig.

'It was called George Washington. It was written in gold on its side.'

'George Washington was the man who never told a lie,' said Brock.

'Well, that was my engine,' said Sam.

After tea he unpacked the basket and distributed the presents to the wondering family.

'Here's a blue bonnet with roses that never die for you, Sister Ann,' said he.

'Oh, Sam darling!' cried little Ann, and she perched the child's bonnet on her head and ran out to the stream to look at herself in the water.

'Here's a frying-pan for Tom, and seven hand-kerchiefs for Bill,' continued Sam.

'Seven handkerchiefs. One a day,' said Bill.

'And here's a magical ball for Brock, and a frog-mug for me.'

They all looked at the little ship tossing in the sea, with sailors climbing the rigging, and fish swimming in the waters. Then they drank water from the frog-mug and cried out when they saw the green eyes of the frog gazing at them from the bottom.

'And I got a present for Sally the Mare,' said Sam, taking the last parcel out of the basket.

It was a funny flat hat with a tiny pointed crown and two holes for Sally's ears.

'A sun-hat for Sally to wear in the hayfield. They are all the fashion on the best farms, I was told,' said Sam importantly. 'I shall take it to Sally tomorrow.'

'It has been a grand day, a champion day,' said Sam, as he sat in the bath-tub and scrubbed off the layers of coal dust that night. 'If only I needn't have had a bath, it would have been a perfect day.'

'How much money did you take?' asked Brock.

'Only the penny with a hole in it,' said Sam, 'and I brought it back again. It's my lucky penny.'

358

87

Who is he?

His name is Smudge, and he's the mascot of the Junior Puffin Club.

What is that?

It's a Club for children between 4 and 8 who are beginning to discover and enjoy books for themselves.

How does it work?

On joining, members are sent a Club badge and Membership Card, a sheet of stickers, and their first copy of the magazine, *The Egg*, which is sent to them four times a year. As well as stories, pictures, puzzles and things to make, there are competitions to enter and, of course, news about new Puffins.

For details of cost and an application form, send a stamped addressed envelope to:

The Junior Puffin Club
Penguin Books Limited
Bath Road
Harmondsworth
Middlesex UB7 ODA